Amber – Eager
By Lilian Middleton
Copyright © 2024 by Lilian Middleton

This work of fiction has changed dates, details and personnel while still paying tribute to the brave members of the Air Transport Auxiliary as part of this novel.

Also by Lilian Middleton:

ARABELLA
TALES FROM THE DISPENSING BENCH
THE PEARL EARRINGS

AMBER

Eager for the Air

For my dear daughter Helen, Brave, Strong & Caring

CHAPTER 1
AMBER

The aircraft taxied to its allotted parking bay, cut its engines, then the steps were rolled into place. The passengers flowed down them with easy grace they were mainly young women and older men setting foot in England for the first time.

Their clothes were almost uniform. Neatly pressed, tan-coloured slacks were topped with cream or tan rolled-neck sweaters, and leather jackets. Their boots and shoes were of the same high-quality leather.

A keen observer would have noticed that one of the women's slacks were neatly creased and her sweater was cashmere while her jacket was warmly lined.

She was not conventionally beautiful but there was about her an air of self-confidence. She knew her worth and trusted her judgement and abilities. Though lacking her mother's brilliant eyes, hers were fine and far-seeing, used to searching the horizon. Her hair was that unusual mixture of several colour strands which no hairdresser however skilled, could achieve with dyes. Glowing amber her mother called it.

Her American accent was less pronounced than that of her fellows for she was from the East Coast of America, and having an English mother, held dual citizenship.

On the flight over the passengers had enquired about each other's backgrounds. The one thing they held in common was that they were all highly qualified pilots and were to assist Britain in her desperate fight against Germany, the old formidable foe.

Amber Seymour used her mother's maiden name, for her real surname marked her out as a member of one of America's richest and most powerful families.

Buses waited for the passengers to take them to a reception centre where they would stay until processed.

The word seemed to cover a multitude of procedures which had begun for the girls back home when they were recruited, interviewed, and accepted for their great adventure, by the inspiring and indefatigable Jacqueline Cochran.

With her application forms completed, Amber had waited for the result expecting to be sent to Montreal for medicals and initial training. Instead, she had been recalled for a further interview with one of Miss Cochran's senior staff. "We are astonished at the extent of your experience flying such a large number of planes for Grantley Aeronautical Group. Were these all planes in development, and when did you begin flying for Grantley's?"

"Initially Ma'am I learned to fly out of a huge interest. As my skills reached advanced level I was trusted to assess and report on developing aircraft. I have very acute hearing and often 'felt' a problem though I'm unsure quite how but needed to report accurately. A family member had allowed me to fly with her from age 12 I guess, as I'd plagued her for years."

"I note that you have dual American/English citizenship. I could send you direct to England to join the existing Air Transport Auxiliary British girls and fast-track you. However, as you have spent your life in America, I would be happier for you to travel to Montreal and complete your training with those flyers going out with the first group. Much of it will seem basic to you. I know you will have the good sense to keep that fact and the huge number of hours you have flown, to yourself. Details will follow and I wish you good luck."

Amber had completed her basic training and had succeeded in hiding both her irritation and huge experience.

Now she was boarding an English bus in the land of her birth. Arabella had told her daughter about Courtneys, the house and estate where she had grown up. It had played such a central part in Arabella's life.

Arrogantly her daughter, who was a true Yankee with little interest in her roots, had paid no attention.

Strange then that Amber had opted to leave her comfortable home in America for England. Perhaps her roots went deeper than she realised. Perhaps it was the challenge of flying in wartime conditions, even though not in combat.

The future looked mighty interesting.

CHAPTER 2
ARABELLA

Amber's mother Arabella Seymour had grown up at Courtneys the country estate where her mother was housekeeper.

She had spent her early years in the nursery with Richard & Caroline Courtney. Her first job was as a lowly maid there.

It was her outstanding 'voice, determination, and beauty which had elevated her to international fame as a consummate opera star. While touring in America she had met and bewitched Francis Grantley heir to the fabulously wealthy Grantley Corporation.

Francis supported his wife in every way, accepting her absences on tour from the family home Fairhaven with good grace.

He applauded her purchase of Courtneys, caused by the excesses and dereliction of Richard Courtney. Francis's wealth helped to restore her home.

Here their daughter Amber had been born. With war clouds looming, Francis's family visited England for Amber's first birthday celebrations. During the visit, Dorothea Grantley was forging a strong bond with her granddaughter. Amber was always happier with Dorothea talking quietly to her and showing her the flowers and birds as she wheeled the child's pram around the garden.

Dorothea had no doubt of Arabella's love for her son. Yet spending so much time at Courtneys when Francis was in America, he was denied the comfort of his wife and child.

Dorothea urged Arabella "You must join us in America, for it is unthinkable for Francis to face the increasing demands of the Grantley Corporation with a huge ocean separating him from you both, for who knows how many years? He yearns for you when you are apart, and fears for your safety in wartime England."

Arabella could not readily admit that she would feel the same devastation when separated from the golden stones and green acres of Courtneys. How could she bear it? Yet bear it she must, for Amber needed to be with both her parents. The war effort needed Francis and Francis needed her and Amber. With no excuse and a heavy heart Arabella set about the task of closing down her life at Courtneys.

CHAPTER 3
<u>AMBER</u> – America here I come

The child sat peaceably on a blanket set between the chairs of her parents on the deck of the liner carrying them all to New York. The occasional clash of her bricks and other toys did little to disturb the placid sunlit day.

Arabella, shaded by a large sunhat and dark glasses had given Nanny Beecham an extended afternoon break from her tawny-haired daughter. Amber had proved to be such a demanding baby. Her protracted and difficult birth seemed to have affected the child, who screamed in frustration, spat out any food she disliked, and was generally difficult. Arabella expected the separation from her friend Eddy and his dog Flossie at their English estate, Courtneys, would result in major tantrums. However, Amber surprised her parents by settling into the routine of the great ship quite calmly.

Alerted by a silence at her side Arabella glanced at her daughter, only to see an empty blanket, "Francis wake up she said urgently Where is Amber? Has nanny collected her?" Shaking his head he rose from the chair "I'll go left – you go right. She can't have got too far crawling, and someone must have noticed her."

Anxious enquires produced no positive response until a lady

remembered a child toddling confidently past.

So it was that her parents missed Ambers's first steps. The child smiled happily at her relieved parents once they had been reunited. She became positively sunny as she discovered her new game of hide and seek and became expert at it. It was a relief for Francis, Arabella, and Nanny Beecham when the party disembarked in New York.

For the heir to a great fortune, the Grantley Corporation swung into action. The family left their stateroom accompanied by a senior officer of the line. By the time they had thanked and bidden farewell to the captain, their immediate luggage was already loaded on the several cars awaiting them at the quayside, and they were whisked away.

Francis and his mother had been tasked with finding a new home for Arabella and Amber now that they were moving to America permanently. As they were driven through New York City the old bustle, energy, and excitement of such vitality hit Arabella anew. What a vibrant nation America had become, fueled by its huge natural resources, and determined immigrants.

Their new home was 10 miles outside the city limits. New Horizons stood, recently built, in its own large grounds. It was built on a rise to give fine views of the gardens, grounds, and woodlands. Its angles, huge floor to ceiling glass windows and stark white walls were in total contrast to the ancient golden stones and serenity of Courtneys.

It would not prove a restful house, as it collected the sun and wind within the uneven facades. Arabella disliked it at once but turned a smiling face on her husband and thanked him for finding them a 'modern' home as she had requested.

Dorothea had interviewed and appointed a start-up staff for her and they had attended to Francis during the weeks he had lived there. Nanny was delighted and relieved that it included two experienced nursery maids. Amber very soon gave them the slip until discovered in the large laundry basket. Soon her daily hide and seek disappearances had everyone on edge.

Her anxious parents reviewed some of her hiding places: the dog kennel, behind the apple store shelves, hidden in the stable where Francis kept his horse, having scaled the door and totally unafraid of being trodden on, upstairs under her parent's bed, in Nanny's wardrobe, under a blanket in the back of her father's car. An extra, younger nursery maid was appointed with the sole duty of becoming Amber's minder. Having been given the slip it was her prompt action which discovered her charge sitting contently in the back of a delivery van leaving the house and munching an apple.

It simply couldn't go on.

Amber had been slow to speak. Mama & Papa did not feature in her vocabulary. One word did and frequently: 'Wing-Want-Wing.'

Arabella remembered the coal black foal born at the Courtney stud, sired by its great stallion Raven.

Eddy the son of Arabella's former dresser Bridie, was Amber's constant companion and would wheel Amber's pram down to the paddock where Wing would nuzzle Amber's hand as she reached out to him and laughed in delight.

Francis ordered a pony as near to Wing as he could get. Amber at once fell in love with her new companion, christened him Wing, and was always to be found in the future with her beloved pony. Success and relief at last for her parents.

Amber listened carefully to her riding instructor becoming a correct and elegant rider. She insisted on being closely involved in Wing's care, although much too young to undertake the heavy work.

Soon she was regularly a fierce competitor in the many gymkhanas. Her groom Micky tried to dissuade her from entering open classes, but his wilful charge would often override him and compete against much larger horses and older riders. As she was tall for her age, few objected. Amber moved seamlessly to a bigger Wing whose luxury stable, tack room, and groom's room were festooned with rosettes of every size and colour.

She now attended a 'Day school for young ladies' as her parents wished to keep some contact and control over their daughter. Amber had always turned first to Nanny, one of the nursemaids or her father for comfort. Amber seemed to view her mother as a distant figure to be treated with some indifference.

War had broken out in Europe as her father had predicted. Francis was often tired and distracted, Amber's safe and secure world seemed unaffected even when Micky her groom joined the draft and was replaced by an older man.

As the war tore Europe apart, so too was Amber's world set to explode in a most unexpected way.

CHAPTER 4
ALL CHANGE

Amber loved to ride Wing in the estate woodlands weaving among the trees with Micky keeping an eye on his young charge, While he paused to light a cigarette, she steered Wing smartly into a well-hidden grove smiling happily to herself. Suddenly she was plucked from her horse and a hand clasped over her mouth.

How dare anyone treat her so and spoil her ride? Instinctively she bit into the hand and bit hard and deeply, for there were no half measures with this girl. The bitten one bellowed in pain. Before he could react, she had sprung back onto Wing and launched the horse at her would be assailant, screaming like an Irish banshee before turning on the second man who now tried to throw a blanket over her head. A deft poke to his eyes with her crop sent him flying. Alerted by the shouting and screaming Micky now appeared, seized Wing's bridle, and fled with her.

The police only found automobile tracks and no sign of her would-be kidnappers. From now on she was accompanied by two grooms, both armed and was restricted to open ground. Had her assailants succeeded the ransom demanded for the Grantley heiress would have been phenomenal. Let alone the risk to her life.

The wretched war and now this!

When Francis held Arabella's hand and gravely told her that he was leaving to join the American troops now pouring into Europe she knew that it would be useless to protest. Such was his knowledge of pre-war Germany and her armaments, his advice on what was needed for the allies to improve their progress was urgently required.

Amber thought her father looked very smart in his uniform with his honorary high rank and waved enthusiastically as he left her and her mother.

There could be no question but that they would be safer and better guarded at the Fairhaven Grantley estate which Dorothea and Randolph had established as the large family compound. Over the years it had become home to their many family members. It was luxuriously equipped as befitted their status. Arabella and Amber now joined them.

It was so exciting for Amber to live with Grandma Dorothea, Grandpa Randolph and all the aunts and uncles. She could take Wing and Micky and even Nanny whom she was far too grown up to need with her.

Arabella felt only gratitude to be leaving 'New Horizons.' Apart from supporting her husband, renewing their marriage, and bringing up Amber she had felt bereft there.

Her once enviable career had declined into gala charity performances and appearing with Dorothea at charity events.
She was still much photographed but was now captioned as 'The elegant and beautiful Mrs Francis Grantley' rather than the once very famous 'Arabella.'

Changes were needed – and soon.

CHAPTER 5
FAIRHAVEN

Amber's favourite word became adore. She adored her new home with so many relatives to fuss over her and pet her. Here there were dogs everywhere and more horses and ponies, But not one as great as Wing. Micky rode out with her on the constantly patrolled huge estate.

Arabella felt foolish to have rejected this lovely warm and safe home. Amber was blossoming with so much attention and company.

Only Arabella's fears for Francis's safety as the war dragged on, and her yearning for England, clouded her days.

It was Dorothea who out of the blue came to her rescue.

"My dear you must renew your own interests. Amber is becoming so very busy with her riding and competitions, that you have the opportunity to sing again."

"Well, my old impresario Hugh has never stopped asking me to do so. He wants me to take a short course of lessons, and then undertake a tour of major cities.

He assures me that it will be a complete sell out as he publicises the return of the great Arabella, while not withholding my Grantley connections. Do you mind Dorothea?"

"Far from it my dear. Your music will reinvigorate you and help you to forget your concerns in the excitement of your performances. Francis would approve."

And so, it happened as Hugh had predicted and Amber waved her mother off enthusiastically and without a jot of regret.

Arabella found herself swept up once again into her old life as an opera star, she had always completed her daily vocal exercises and found her voice responded to her lessons and regular usage. Hugh arranged her new costume fittings and even engaged her former dresser Maire Quinlan who had settled in America before the wretched war. America was the land of the free and, free from any war on its shores, with an insatiable demand for entertainment.

As Hugh had promised, her tour was an enormous success. The press were only too happy to report on the very stylish Arabella, with added emphasis on the Grantley corporation's wealth, and its patriotic production of arms for the boys on overseas duties.

There was something so tender and endearing in Arabella's performances. At 37 her beauty of face and figure had matured. Her gowns were always simple but of the finest quality with a hair ornament to accessorise. Her sincerity shone through her new programme. Hugh had assisted her as they mulled over her recital repertoire. They bore in mind that she now attracted a younger audience, with many of the men wearing uniforms. To cater for changing tastes, she now sang fewer arias and church music. There was an enthusiastic response to patriotic songs lauding 'our boys over there.' The biggest variations were for sentimental songs which really were not well enough written for her range. She sang what would please her audience, and was well rewarded by the ovations, floral gifts, and the ensuing press reports which ensured 'house full' notices.

It was gratifying to be earning her own money again rather than relying on Francis. Money earned by her own efforts reminded her of the early days as she fought to find the funds to purchase Courtneys.

CHAPTER 6
AMBER

Amber missed her absent mother, not one teeny bit. She knew full well that both her parents loved her, yet she found Arabella a little cool and distant in a way she felt but would have found hard to explain. It was as though some central core was just icy and even the combined talents of Amber and Francis could not melt it. With Francis also gone, the girl put her total love, trust, and adoration on to her grandmother. Dorothea was the ideal choice. She seldom admonished Amber too severely when she behaved outrageously.

"Come my dear that is not the standard of behaviour I expect. If you must shout and rage, please take yourself off to a private corner. There you can stamp your foot and recover yourself. Also do not use the language you sometimes hear from your grandfather. It is inappropriate for a young lady."

In the face of a grandmother's quiet calm, and not wanting to upset her, Amber also became less restless and demanding.

With her move to Fairhaven another great and wonderful event occurred. It was now too far to travel to her former day school. It was agreed that boarding school would be too frustrating for it would separate her from her energetic outdoor life. So it was that Mrs Juliet Adams entered Amber's world as her governess.

The previous mysteries of mathematics became less mysterious once clearly explained and understood. Mrs Adams made it clear that numeracy was so very important at every stage of life. Take time and trouble with the basics and all else was understandable. If you knew your time's tables backward-quite literally-the answers flew into your head.

Teaching was skilfully done; knowledge assimilated much respect established and under a timetable which allowed a comprehensive education posted. The Grantley heiress would need much knowledge, assorted skills and abundant common sense. Amber now had a solid base by which to achieve these objectives.

Amber mixed with likeminded and highly competitive children at the gymkhanas, making new friends and some foes. She mixed freely with the Fairhaven staff with no attention to her status.

On one great occasion, Dorothea and her aunts took her to New York. They shopped in Bloomingdale's and the great stores as women do. Amber bore the indignity of trying on girly dresses with good grace, and a new riding habit with enthusiasm. She was unaware that they were at all times followed by two burly escorts. She was to be allowed to attend the theatre for the first time. Suitably attired in her new blue velvet dress with a matching ribbon in her vibrant hair and black patent pumps, she took her seat in a prominent box. The orchestra played a merry overture, and the red velvet curtains opened smoothly.

On stage stood a black grand piano shining like Wing when she had just groomed him. Her eyes were drawn from the pianist to the beautiful woman bathed in the spotlights. She wore the most perfect golden dress, a diamante headdress but no other jewellery. As she began to sing Amber felt the hairs on her neck tingle. Could the golden creature be her mother?

At the song's end, Amber stood up to clap her hands until the palms hurt. Now at last she knew what her mother did, where she gave her love and passion and sympathies. Ambers's understanding was unusually perceptive.

The small party was allowed to visit Arabella during the interval, Amber flew into her mother's arms and covered her with kisses. With that exchange mother and daughter were reconnected as Amber at last knew her mother's worth.

With all her activities and enthusiasms Amber had failed to notice that Dorothea seemed a little quiet and preoccupied. When Arabella made her longed for return to Fairhaven at the end of her engagements, she too seemed a little sad though she claimed tiredness.

One Sunday Amber found her grandfather alone in the garden.

"Grandpa I know something is wrong, but no one will tell me what. You can trust me you know. I so hate it when Mama and Grandma and now you are so sad. Please tell me for I'm old enough to bear bad news."

Struck by the maturity of his granddaughter, Randolph agreed that she should know. "The reason my dear is that we have not received any letters from your father for several months. He wrote regularly from France, but we are so concerned. I've been in touch with the government to try and find him, for he was on a mission for the war department. Still no news, but we're onto it." "Thank you for telling me said Amber gravely. It's better I know so now they need not whisper or change the subject. But Grandpa, Micky says the war will soon be over, and all our boys will soon be back surely Papa will be with them?"

"I surely hope so," said Randolph. "Now run along and tell granny that I need some coffee very soon."

Amber carried the message to Dorothea, then caught hold of her hand and said" I know about Papa. He'll be fine, I know

24

it for he would never leave Mama and me ever." "Of course, he wouldn't my dear. There will be some good reasons for his letters to be delayed."

Dorothea smiled reassuringly at Amber, but her shrewd granddaughter saw the fear in her eyes.

The months until the longed for Armistice dragged by with no news of Francis or his fellow officers. They had simply disappeared without trace.

CHAPTER 7
ARABELLA

The euphoria which greeted the end of the Great War saw a wave of relief sweep America. Joy was unconfined. The date of the signing of the Armistice was known to Randolph and his fellow industrialists well before November 11th.

The total surrender of Germany was to be slowly followed by the return of the American boys. Their fitness, valour, and superior arms - many of which had been manufactured by Grantley industries and had swung the war in favour of exhausted French and British armies. Australian, Canadian, and other Empire troops had fought valiantly.

Arabella drew on all her acting skills to join the celebrations. At heart, she wondered - Great War - what was great about it? Great loss of life with so many slaughtered on all sides. The loss of a generation of fine young men. A generation of women who could never marry with sweethearts dead, the sadness that Francis was still unaccounted for bore down on her. Was she now a widow? What was her future? All she knew was that it did not lie in America despite her welcome into the heart of Francis's family, and their care and respect. Fairhaven was never, or could ever be, home. To Courtneys, she must return to heal her spirit. Instinctively she knew that Amber was so taken up with her life and many interests that she would wish to stay in America so be it!

It was Randolph, tired out by the demands of the huge

conglomerate he headed, and the loss of his son, who came to her rescue.

"I understand my dear. I too felt the magic of Courtneys, even on just one visit. May I present you with a ticket for one of the first boats to resume sailing to Europe? It won't be as luxurious as usual, but comfortable at least."

Arabella did what unnerves all strong men and burst into tears of gratitude and relief. "Now, now my dear, this isn't like you. Dry your eyes and get busy it always helps, and there isn't much time left before you sail."

Arabella found her daughter at the stables where she greeted her mother with a jaunty 'Hi Mom' and a kiss. How American our daughter was. "My dear I need to talk to you. We've spoken of this before. You've visited the school and now will be a good time for you to go there. You need to be with girls of your own age. You will start after Christmas as a weekly boarder and return here on Friday afternoons."

"Yep, I guess you're right. I'm quite looking forward to beating them at all the sports," was her daughter's confident reply.

"I'm sorry darling, but I have to return to England, Courtneys, and the people there need me after this long, long war. At least I know that your grandparents will look out for you. Enjoy your school and all the friends you will make. I'll write and telegraph, and we can enjoy our last few days together."

"OK Mom. Gotta go now to exercise Wing. See you later."

CHAPTER 8
RETURN TO COURTNEYS

Arabella realised that her days of so much privilege and acclaim would soon be over. Returning to an England decimated by a cruel war would be different from her current situation, and what would she find at Courtneys?

The news that, in common with many country estates, Courtneys had been chosen to become an officer's convalescent home, was still startling.

It was obvious by late 1915 that long exposure to brutal warfare was claiming officers who had led the endless charges and were suffering from shell shock and other mental problems. There was an army doctor in charge with an assistant doctor and several orderlies, both nursing and organising activities and treatments. Others had taken over the kitchens and only Maggie, Micky, a maintenance man and a maid of all work remained. They in turn had moved to the flats over the extensive stables where they were soon joined by that old head gardener, Archibald Finch. Here he could be assured of company, meals, cleaning, and laundry service and most importantly the company of the Courtney stud's great stallion, Raven. At 17 Raven was too old to stand as sire, and also very thankfully, for war service. The young pretender Wing who had won Amber's heart as a baby was safely stabled in the woods to avoid any conscripting officer and to maintain the lineage of the black Courtney horses - after the wretched war. Micky was determined that the horse would not become cannon fodder.

Arabella received the sad news that Raven had died in his box in September 1918. By October of that year, Finch had followed suit, deprived of 'the great black hoss' he had helped to save, and its companionship.

Old Finch had always threatened 'Ah'll drop off me perch in that dang gret garden what ah've laboured in most o' me life. Ah expect as ow you'll shove me under in that dratted rose patch, so it'll be me old bones as'll fertilise 'em. Bet you'll get cabbage size roses that'll all smell as sweet as what I do.'

Arabella could not help smiling at the image of her old gardener crouched in the branches of one of his trees ready to 'drop off' and no doubt snatching two of the golden apples to share with Raven when they were reunited.

Like many of his generation, he believed in a just God who would look kindly on his servant, hopefully overlooking the times when Finch had drunk a little too heavily at The Fox and rolled back to his cottage in an inebriated state.

Courtneys gardens had bloomed and yielded their bounty at his touch.

Quite an Epitaph.

Contrary to his prediction he was not buried in the dratted rose patch, but by special dispensation alongside Raven at the edge of the trees next to the main paddock.

His mourners returned to the Fox Inn, and the wake was as celebratory as Finch would have liked, except Miss Arabella and Finch himself weren't there to sing a duet together.

Wing had been rescued from his woodland sanctuary once he was safe from the equine recruiting officer. Among the recovering officers were several fine horsemen, all eager to ride a horse from the famed Courtney stud.

And what a horse! He would earn his weight in stud fees once England began to recover.

Arabella was on her way to help her country however she could. Her liner showed signs of its great days before serving as a troop carrier, but she cared little, being so impatient to return home that the journey passed in an agony of anticipation.

She was driven not to Courtneys but to the Dower house. There was still too many officers awaiting discharge from the Services living at the big house.

Maggie Jones, her stalwart house manager, waited to greet her. The traditional tea and toast were served by Jenny, the new maid, appointed along with cook by Maggie.

"Oh Maggie, I can't begin to tell you what a relief it is to be back home now that this vile war has at last ended. Your reports have been a lifeline to keep me connected to Courtneys, and what has been happening here. Please tell me every detail of what I can expect when I visit tomorrow." Maggie smiled in her old contained manner. "I'm afraid that would take until tomorrow. Will 10:30 am be convenient? I'll introduce you to Major Spiller and leave him to escort you around."

With that agreed, Arabella was free to kick off her shoes, sit in the garden despite the chill air, and try to contain her longing, for just one more day.

She had been fortunate that the Dower House was available to her. Lady Cynthia Courtney and her daughter Caroline had moved into her son's home Fox Hollie following his death.

The Dower House was a little shabby but extremely clean and comfortable. The next morning was fine and unusually warm for late Autumn. Arabella persuaded herself that it was the estate's way of welcoming her home. How fanciful and so unlike her usual practical nature.

Arabella had dressed with extra care, choosing a smart suit, a warm blouse, sensible shoes, and no hat. As she walked across the park, Courtneys slowly came into view. Her heart leapt! Oh, its indestructible beauty, with its pillared porch and proud chimneys. The windows shone in the low sunlight and winked at her with glee.

She was prepared for some wartime neglect and dilapidation, but all was pristine. The door brasses and bell push shone as they had done in the days when she was responsible for cleaning them as a lowly housemaid.

Maggie Jones answered the bell and conducted Arabella through to what had been her own small sitting room before her departure to America in 1913.

A tall, distinguished man in army officer uniform stood at once to greet her. They exchanged a firm handshake as Maggie made the introductions.

"Mrs Grantley, we meet at long last. It has been a great privilege to work here among such calmness and beauty. I am absolutely confident that Courtneys has contributed greatly to the recovery of many of my patients. They have all respected your home. Would you care to look round? We are slowly winding down, but I would like you to see something of our work here."

"I would be delighted" Arabella responded, "and to reacquaint myself after such a long absence."

"Many of the first editions and my great Audubon 'Birds of America' folio, are in storage. However, I see that you have added to the remaining volumes." Arabella told him.

"Reading is hugely popular and calming. Some of our patients have to be persuaded out of here for mealtimes, and the more active parts of their treatments."

The drawing room was used for general chatting and relaxation while the dining room had been divided into dining and games areas.

The kitchens seemed a little more battered but would respond to coats of cream paint and some up to date American-inspired red equipment. The army cooks seemed efficient and obviously enjoyed their positions.
"That all seems very satisfactory, Major Spiller. Will you tell me something of your treatment methods?"

"Of course – I'll order coffee, and it's warm enough to take it in the little garden pavilion if you would enjoy that?"

Arabella felt a burst of longing for Francis and the many

wonderful times they had spent together. It was there that he had always presented her with a charming jewel when he arrived back at Courtneys. Who could resist a handsome rich and generous husband?

Certainly not Arabella!

With coffee presented and poured, Major Spiller began —

"Our work involves trying to restore badly damaged officers. It was recognised that their scars were not always visible. Many had seen horrible slaughter and been in constant danger. The calm aura of Courtneys, the gardens, stables, woods, and farms so impressed the billeting officer charged with finding houses where our patients could recuperate, that he requisitioned it, as you know.

I was appointed to take charge and set up the medical facility. It was important that the house remain as a relaxing home environment.

The treatment rooms were set up in the stables and carriage houses. It has worked wonderfully well. My treatment methods were regarded as progressive in as much as some military personnel regarded shell shock as nothing more than a dishonourable way of escaping from duty. Also, some medics thought that cold water or electric shock treatment and even complete anaesthesia were to be applauded and used."

Arabella was most impressed and asked several questions about the treatments. She expressed her gratitude that the house was in good order.

"It is part of their characters to be disciplined and orderly. Also, you will find that our patients like physical exercise. Many have experience of farming and of large gardens. Each day we drop them off at the estate farms, where their efforts have helped, as so many of your workers were away fighting."

"Others worked the gardens here. Mr Finch was a hard and entertaining taskmaster, there was much yarning and singing, and I suspect not a little drinking in the bothy. Maggie Jones enjoyed joining in too."

"It proved an important part of their healing. To have your hands in the soil, and experience new growth and beauty, instead of death has been marvellous. I notice that the incidence of nightmares has reduced substantially."

"We have been able to send some to desk jobs in England, a few back to the war, and some discharged. They have all benefited from their time here and we are all so grateful."

Arabella found herself impressed by both the man and the

work he had led.

Rising gracefully, she thanked him before leaving to take a tour of her gardens with Maggie.

All was in the most impeccable order, tended by gardeners wearing a mixture of army and casual gardening clothes. The winter digging had been completed; the greenhouses were in good repair with clean glass. As Arabella and Maggie spoke to the men, they felt justly proud of the help and strength which each attributed to Courtneys gardens. Archibald Finch must have felt the same under his gruff exterior.

It was chastening to find a long list of names pinned to one of the shed doors. Here Finch had kept a note of all the estate lads who had been killed in action, together with the date, and their jobs on the estate. It made sombre reading, and Arabella knew that her estate manager would have a Book of Remembrance for them all. How were they ever to be replaced once all the officers had left?

"Maggie, would you like to join me at the Dower House for supper tonight? I'm seeing John Jarvis tomorrow and there may be questions you wish me to put to him."

"Thank you" replied Maggie. "I am otherwise engaged, but free tomorrow afternoon if you need me."

They passed amicably, but Arabella wondered who Maggie was otherwise engaged with. Her devotion to the gardens and then assuming management of the house had been all-consuming.

Arabella's meeting with John Jarvis was both enlightening and challenging.

"We've kept afloat with all the women taking on the jobs which their men folk did. They have been wonderfully resilient, but I sense that several of them are exhausted. Also, almost every family has lost someone, and they had to work through their grief. The officers from Courtneys have proved a godsend, experienced and physically able. We all knew this could change in an instant. It was not unusual to find one curled up with arms over their heads and tears of fear on their faces. Most wanted to be left alone to recover. Some responded to one of the older women talking to them quietly in motherly tones."

"I'm anxious what will happen when they leave. Too few of our men will return from the war, and we must have financial help in place for the families of our lads who have been killed or badly wounded. Our great advantage will be that we can offer superior wages, thanks to Mr Grantley's generosity. Our produce has earned good prices during the war. It might be wise to grow more arable and root crops and reduce the dairy herds. I'll take some advice and perhaps we can all discuss it when Mr Grantley returns."

"There is still no news of him and several others. The Americans have set up a special team to search for them. They can't have totally disappeared."

Yet it seemed they had. Francis and twelve other senior Americans could not be traced.

Major Spiller met Arabella daily in the weeks before Christmas. They had much to discuss for the many arrangements to be made as the military recovery home prepared to close down with the removal of so much equipment, and the disposal of its patients.

Arabella changed into her usual Courtney outfit, straight skirt, pretty blouse, high heeled shoes, and simple jewellery. She awaited her guest impatiently having invited Major Spiller to the Dower House for supper.

Arabella had come to enjoy his company, his intelligence and his interests which extended well beyond his medical career.

They had discovered a shared enthusiasm for art, and Arabella was happy to describe the great portraits in the Fairhaven collection. He became absorbed in the many other American galleries she had visited. His mother had been a noted water colourist, and he had been encouraged to follow suit. However, his calling had always been medicine.

Arabella found herself in a turmoil. Was she a widow? Had she any right to be sharing time with this very attractive man who was the first to raise in her a frisson of desire after so many years? She had rigorously stopped herself from showing any improper thoughts or flirtatious behaviour. Her innate good taste had resulted in good local food simply cooked, a bottle of decent wine and a table bedecked with candles and simple flowers.

"I thought we deserved to spoil ourselves a little," she told him. "You'll soon be leaving, and I'll miss our times together, so very much."

After supper, Major Spiller regarded her gravely.

"My orders arrived today. The last patients leave on Thursday, and I follow on Saturday. I can officially hand your home back to you then."

Arabella looked at him with undisguised dismay. "But you can't be leaving so soon she exclaimed." "It's almost Christmas."

"The War Office wants everyone who is fit enough to be home with their families. They'll all benefit. I'll thank you formally and ceremoniously return the keys at 12 noon on Saturday. You know how very much your friendship and encouragement have meant to me. I'll never forget you

Arabella."

This was the first time that Robert had ever used her Christian name. She saw in his eyes such unmistakable longing and flung herself into his arms. Their first kiss was full of sweetness, and almost despair. Too late to become star-crossed lovers, too much loyalty to the absent Francis and Robert's wife Sarah. Ever the officer and gentleman he stepped back, wiped the tears from her huge violet eyes, kissed her again, then bowed and left her disconsolate.

At least on Saturday, they could shake hands on his departure with dignity, but
oh, the regrets. She had wanted so badly to take him to her bed!

The house and gardens seemed so quiet and lifeless without the officers and staff. To distract them all Arabella and Maggie Jones held a 'Council of War.' What were they to do about Christmas 1918? There should have been rejoicing at the return of Courtneys to the family and the end of the war.

Both agreed that their usual celebrations were unrealistic with so few days to go.

Arabella had received an invitation to stay with Christopher and Laura Richards and Maggie would go home to Lincolnshire. Micky the only remaining 'live-in' retainer had friends in the village.

Two of the orderlies had asked to remain at Courtneys and to work there, Maggie thought them both capable and reliable, so generator, boiler and security would be covered.

The New Year must bring news of Francis. The uncertainty was draining. Randolph would surely find his son.

CHAPTER 9
SILENT KILLER

The great catastrophe which struck so soon after the Great War was an unseen enemy. Its killer reach respected no one, man, woman or child. Its progress was inexorable and lethal. It came to be known in world history as the Spanish Flu.

The peoples of Europe, weakened by years of war fell before it. Soldiers who had survived untold days and privation to return home to safety, now found that safety was an illusion. The disease was not selective. As long as it could proliferate and spread and replicate, it did so.

The returning troops carried it to America, Canada, India, Australia and China. A single unguarded sneeze could lay low a dozen people. Neither was there any rhyme nor reason as to who recovered and who died.

Amber knew none of this, only that she was prevented from seeing her Grandmother. That lady was now nursing her Grandpa Randolph. True, he was worn down by the demands of his great businesses as Grantley Industries had worked flat out to supply the American armies fighting in Europe. True, he was desperate to discover the fate of his only son.

Randolph's two daughters were rightly advancing the

interests of motors and aeroplanes, which would take up the extra production available now that the armament sections were wound down.

His doctors were optimistic. Randolph was well nourished and had an all-compassing determination. Alas, they were wrong. Randolph's great heart ceased to beat at last. The Founder and dynamo of the great corporation he headed was dead.

Dorothea kept to her rooms for several days both mourning her charismatic husband and to ensure she was not infected. Then she emerged to take charge of Randolph's funeral and with her calmness and compassion, care for all the family.

Amber kept her tears and upset to herself but was deeply distraught. With her father lost in Europe and her mother permanently in England, Randolph and Dorothea had in effect become her parents as well as grandparents. She was bereft.

Randolph's death was not only a personal loss to his family.

He was a good industrialist, a symbol of the American dream where a man of high energy and intelligence could create and head a vast, conglomerate of businesses, that led the world.

The tributes poured in. The great and the good from the President down sent their condolences. Because of the raging flu epidemic, Randolph's funeral was a private service for family and those of his employees who were prepared to take the risk of attending.

Life at Fairhaven during the epidemic could never again be so carefree for Amber. She missed her grandfather greatly and saw the sadness which never left Dorothea's eyes, despite her soft smile.

The lawyers seemed always to be visiting for conferences with Dorothea, the aunts and board members. With Francis still unaccounted for, major decisions must be taken, and huge sums of money were involved.

To her chagrin, Amber became a source of constant conjecture in the newspapers, where she was frequently referred to as the 'Golden Girl of Grantleys.'

Efforts to discover Francis – or his fate – redoubled or the time must pass before he was declared as presumed dead, and his sisters could take full control of the business on Amber's behalf.

Predators soon gathered hoping to reduce Grantley's industrial might and buy sections at heavily discounted prices. Randolph's legacy was not to be easily lost.

Dorothea was particularly determined to protect Randolph's foresight. He had already started to re-tool, preparing to convert 'swords into ploughshares. Tractors and farming machinery were going to be big worldwide business and Grantley's would be well placed to profit from them.

Family, board members and lawyers agreed to back these plans. Meanwhile, the market for cars would surge post-war with Aunt Phillipa developing new models. The peacetime demands for leisure aircraft meant that Annette's planes were sold almost as soon as they were built and tested.

Francis would return to a thriving business. Dorotha was completely sure of this.

CHAPTER 10
COURTNEYS – The return

Arabella's plans to redecorate and restore her home needed to be revised. There was already a shortage of labour on the estate. The casualties of the war were no longer replaced by the officers recuperating at Courtneys. The additional losses from the Spanish Flu were further weakening the estate.

It was a small enough list to keep Courtneys going. General repairs and refurbishment must join the list and be tackled as and when they could be managed.

Happily, when Arabella moved back into her home, her bedroom/bathroom, small sitting room and drawing room were all glowing and Maggie had adorned them with foliage and some flowers. It so reminded Arabella of her days as housemaid at Courtneys with her mother as housekeeper. Happier and easier times altogether.

There awaited her on her desk a pile of letters and one larger package. It contained many song sheets and a sealed letter.

   Miss Arabella

Ah've knowed you since yer wer a sprog. Your Ma wer a special lass. So, it's only right that yer special an all.

Yer've made us all right proud wi yer singin' It wer the greatest day when I sang wi you, an Mister Francis an all. We won't ever forgit yer workin yer socks off to buy Courneys, an keep us all in work.

Ah just need to warn yer. Ah ears from other gardeners yer know. All these great big fancy houses 'll cost too much to keep goin 'now there aint any heirs to follow on. Them Jerries did for too many. Ah know Mr Francis 'll come back, he's bin wonderful helpin yer to keep it all goin.

Till then if Mr Randolph and the American side don't keep payin, yer'll be in trouble. Keep 'old o' the land even if it int possible to farm it all. It'll be like gold when things pick up. Don't yer let nobody gyp yer or do yer down. Ye'r a bright lass, an money saved is money wot don't ave to be earned. Yer've loved Courtneys and saved it from Mr Richard, so ang on to it wi' all yer might. That little lass o' yourn needs to love it an all.

I'm leavin me gardin notes to Maggie, an all me songs to you an Mister Francis, cos you'll like 'em.

It's bin gret workin for yer.

Keep smilin! Keep singin, an keep smellinin the dang roses.

Your obedient servant

Archbold Finch

Arabella was not easily moved to tears, but the words and advice of her old gardener caused her to weep for all the past, which despite all the problems, seemed so much more hopeful than today.

The news of Randolph's death had hit her hard. Now Finch's words regarding her financial future revived her concerns. Would her allowances continue from Grantley's? Would Francis be declared dead? Would she be a wealthy widow or just another dependent of the Grantley trusts? There was so many unknowns. Meanwhile, she must keep her wits about her and continue with her work cleaning the library ready to reclaim the first edition great Audubon bird book from safe storage.

On a bright, breezy and unusually warm April morning Arabella was feeling more optimistic and dare she admit it – almost happy – as she worked at her desk in the library. The doors were open wide to welcome the warm sunlit day. She became aware of a shadow falling over her books. Looking up she saw a skeletal old man wearing a far too large American officer's uniform and leaning heavily on a walking stick. The man extended a hand to her and said a single word – "Arabella."

She flew to his side and helped him to a comfortable chair. As she knelt beside him and took his hand all she could manage was," Francis, oh Francis." She must never let him see the dismay on her face at his condition only the joy and relief that he had at last returned to her, Amber and Courtneys.

Ringing quickly, she asked for coffee, warm milk brandy and some soft bread and butter.

Francis lay back exhausted in his chair until her soft voice said.

"Sip this my darling," offering him a half cup of warm milk and tiny squares of bread. The milk with just a touch of brandy seemed to revive him a little.

"Can you make it upstairs darling?" she asked.

"I need to sit in the garden pavilion first,"

"Of course," replied Arabella, as she rang for one of the orderlies to help her husband,

"I'll get John Webster. He is experienced and will help you."

With Francis settled and a blanket over his legs Arabella just sat quietly holding his hand.

"Amber?" He questioned.

"Growing up fast at Fairhaven and obsessed with horses and automobiles."

"Ah" he sighed contentedly and fell into a deep and hopefully refreshing sleep.

Arabella examined her husband carefully. His hair was now completely grey. His skin was slack and very pallid, and he was almost skeletally thin, she could feel the bones as she still held his hands.

When Maggie arrived, Arabella put her finger to her lips and whispered.

"We must nurse him back to better health. Ask cook for broths, milk puddings and egg dishes. We can do it Maggie – we must!"

Maggie nodded her agreement and left to ensure that cook would be well prepared. When he awoke, John Webster helped him back into the library, where very small portions of lunch were served to him. As the afternoon dusk fell Arabella realised that he was becoming unsettled.

"Light, light, I must have light."

All the lights and lamps were turned on and were never extinguished in his presence, except in the brightest daylight hours.

Brian Breed, the other orderly, took turns with John Webster to be on duty to assist Francis. Arabella requested an interview with the Grantley London offices to find out the details of her husband's capture and rescue, so as to spare Francis from the many questions she needed to be answered.

Guy Winterton arrived at Courtneys with papers requiring Francis's signature to further confirm his identity and claim as the legitimate heir and new owner of the Grantley Corporation.

Mr Winterton and Arabella then moved to her sitting room.

"Please tell me all you know about his experiences and whereabouts from when he went missing Mr Winterton. It is important I know everything so that I can help his recovery in an informal manner."

The story of inhumanity and suffering that unfolded appalled Arabella, but she dare not show her emotions.

He began –

"Major Grantley was captured with several other officers forming an investigation unit. The Germans realised the importance and probable wealth of their captives. At first, they were well treated as befitted their rank. However, as the war turned against Germany assisted by the new American troops, conditions became more spartan and food scarce. With the unconditional surrender, the Germans should have released the men immediately, but their guards were fanatical and refused to acknowledge Germany's defeat. They moved Francis and his companions into a prison hidden in huge caves. Here they were kept in almost complete darkness for many months. It was the sharp-sighted airman who noticed smoke issuing from an uninhabited hillside on several occasions who saved them. He directed a troop of American soldiers to the site. The guards had, at last, deserted the prisoners but left them securely bolted behind hidden metal doors to await their fate."

"Ten of them had survived to be transferred to a hospital. Your husband was too ill to be questioned. All were suffering from severe malnutrition and lack of essential vitamins and having been kept in darkness. Only the smoke from the small fire they kept going saved them. When Major Grantley was at last able to be repatriated, he asked to come here first, rather than America. Since the unfortunate death of Mr Randolph Grantley, his family have been keeping the business afloat and thriving until Mr Francis is fit enough to resume directing the companies. When might that be Mrs Grantley?"

"My husband is under the care of the local ex-military doctor and two experienced medical orderlies. I have some nursing experience too. His recovery is slowed because he can only take very small amounts of food at one time. We provide very nutritious food at very regular intervals. I could perhaps persuade him to see a specialist. He sleeps well and has no nightmares, just an understandable fear of darkness. It is better that I know all this and what pitfalls to avoid. Please do thank Dorothea and Francis's sisters for their wonderful work, and belief that Francis would indeed return. I'll send you regular information regarding his progress and do realise that for the sake of the business, we have to present a very positive picture."

"Thank you, Mrs Grantley. I see you understand the position perfectly."

With that, Mr Winterton took his leave.

Arabella returned to join Francis in the pavilion when he looked at her expectantly. "I know now what happened to you Francis and why we didn't hear from you. I don't know how you survived so much harshness and fear. Now you are here with me, I'll do absolutely everything I can to help you to get your strength back."

Francis looked at Arabella so lovingly that her heart contracted.

"I survived because of you my darling," he said.

"I just remembered you on a darkened stage with the spotlights showing your beauty. Then I sang along in my mind with your glorious music, and it did indeed 'calm the savage breast.' I lost myself in the joy of your voice and performance and forced the hateful reality aside. One of our number spoke German fluently but did not admit it. He knew what the guards were planning and when the war ended. We never lost hope but were desperate when they abandoned us to certain death until that wonderful airman realised what was unusual about the smoke from our fire."

"No more talking now, dear heart. It's time for your rest," said Arabella.

She was still unsure whether he knew of Randolph's death but must raise the matter. The signing of so many papers this morning must surely have alerted him. Soon the decision must be taken to return to America.

'Not yet she prayed – not yet.'

If remembering her singing had helped to keep him alive during his imprisonment, would it help now?

She took out of the drawer the simple songs left to her and Francis by Archibald Finch. Very quietly she began to hum one of the tunes, then sing the words.

"Come and sit beside me," said Francis before joining his uncertain voice to hers.

As she remembered Archibold Finch, she recalled reaching out for one of his roses as a young girl. Francis who was tutoring the Courtney children had painted her as he hid in the same garden pavilion where they now sat.

On the following day, an easel, canvas, and paints plus a sketchbook and watercolours were set out for him. At first, Francis shook his head but when Arabella returned with drinks and small, sweet biscuits he had almost completed a sketch of Randolph.

"You do know then that your father died in the great flu epidemic. I've been trying to tell you."

"I know and I grieve for him and know that my mother will be distraught. Theirs was a great love, and together they were invincible. As soon as I am strong enough, I must return to her and to Amber. For now, all I need is here at Courtneys my love, with you."

Dorothea had lost her husband and did not intend to lose

her newly liberated son. She and her maid arrived at Courtneys soon after her cable. Arabella was delighted and left them to talk together. His mother held her son's slender hand, smoothed his hair, shared his many drinks and morsels of food, encouraged him to paint, and told him of Amber's exploits, and allowed her calmness and strength to flow into her boy.

With two such formidable women to care for him, Francis began his return to his former self, though never to his original hair colour, nor to his original vigour.

CHAPTER 11

AMBER

Amber had matured greatly since she had last seen her father in 1917 when he went off to war. As she had wept when her grandfather died, so she wept tears of relief when Francis was found alive. Her father was safe and with her mother in England.

Amber set to and wrote letter after letter to them. She might have mentioned her studies occasionally, but always reported on her latest ambition, to be the best driver EVER man or woman. Yes, Amber had discovered a new enthusiasm. It was 'real grand' to drive with her Aunt Phillipa. The development of the automobile and its internal combustion engine had been so completely embraced by that lady that she had persuaded her father Randolph to create a whole new division of the Grantley Corporation, devoted to design and build these 4-wheeled wonders. Phillipa headed   Grantley Automobile Corporation.

She drove with great speed, precision, and utter confidence. Amber sat at her side shaking with excitement and urging the driver to go even faster. "Watch what I do with the gears and pedals Amber, then sit tight and try and copy me. Watch the track and how it banks. When we are on the estate roads you must always look way ahead and be prepared for the unexpected."

As Amber watched her Aunt over the weeks so Amber was obsessed. One day when she visited Philly at the track there was a surprise for her. A brand new scaled-down model especially made by Grantley Automobiles awaited her. It was in vibrant red livery, with a smart mechanic standing alongside. The girl ran her hands over the shining vehicle to get the feel of it. She admired its sleek lines, leather upholstery and sheer quality, with a quiet approval far removed from her noisy style.

Frank her mechanic taught her well. Impatience did not win the day, only solid application and low speeds until he was sure after several lessons that Amber was a safe driver. Although underage, she was free to drive on the estate roads, though always still escorted – she tried not to neglect Wing her horse of course, but heady speed and the modernity of motoring was intoxicating.

Frank also introduced her to the mechanics of motoring, and they loved nothing better than emerging oil-stained and happy after checking an engine as he helped her to detect a fault.

Amber adored her car and christened him CEDRIC, though she never knew why she chose the name. They flew round the circuit together and she sometimes felt that he knew what she was thinking, for they were in such accord. 'I'm definitely going to be a racing driver when I leave school

Frank' she said. With her current progress, he had no reason to doubt her conviction and forward planning.

Amber's life lay before her. Without the larger-than-life figure of Grandpa Randolph. She turned even more to Dorothea when she needed comfort and advice. Amber was tall for her age, with an athletic body used effectively for school sports. Now the five days a week at her school began to drag until the longed for Saturday, which she spent at the track with Philly, Frank and the other drivers and mechanics. Sheer bliss!
Sunday was for morning church and family luncheon, followed by time spent with her Grandmother in the garden.

The news from England of her father's progress was improving. He now replied to her letters and sent her some of the small sketches he made at Courtneys. They included one which she treasured. It was of her mother with head slightly bent in concentration over a book. It encompassed all of Arabella's beauty and style. It was almost as if she would look up and smile at the viewer. Amber had steadfastly resisted any interest in the Fairhaven art collection so dear to her parents. Now she saw how it was possible to capture the character of a person forever. Was there a painting of Randolph she could visit? She must ask Dorothea.

As her birthday approached, Amber grandly stated that she

had everything she needed and would just enjoy Saturday at the track, then her friends and family for a party in the Fairhaven ballroom with a jolly jazz band. It had to be modern at all costs.

Her Aunts Philly and Netty took on the organisation of this great event for their lovely niece. Every decision was ruled by the question 'Will it be fun?' If the answer was 'YES,' then it was to be on the programme for Saturday.

As Amber made her final circuit, she saw a woman standing watching her. Could it be? Was it even possible? She quickly parked her car and sprinted over to her mother. They kissed fondly, and with a jaunty "Hi Mom – it's great to see you – what a fantastic surprise. Where's Pa? How is he?" The fusillade of questions continued without a pause. "Oh darling," said Arabella "Do let me answer." "Your Father is glad – so glad to be home at Fairhaven, he's a little tired, so resting while I collect you. When you see him don't bowl him over like a whirlwind, will you? Take your time to rediscover him after all these years. How you have grown my dear girl."

Arabella found it hard to believe the changes in Amber. Yet when she had removed her helmet and shaken out her glorious hair, she recognised in her daughter a new maturity and sense of responsibility. The three of them met quietly in Francis's room. Amber saw in this slim grey-haired man the father she had always adored. Physically he bore no resemblance to Randolph his impressive father yet exuded the same determination in his own quieter way to return to the life expected of the new owner of Grantley Industries, and to relieve Dorothea of such a heavy burden. They just held hands in easy accord, as he reassured her that he was fine, and wished her all the joys due to his daughter on her birthday.

Dorothea joined them for refreshments in their sitting room. Soon it would be time
to change to welcome their guests for the first great event at Fairhaven since before the Great War.

The lethal pandemic was played out at last, and the world flung itself into the hedonism of what became known as the 'Roaring Twenties.' Fast cars and frolics, new dances, new fashions and new money everywhere made America the centre of fun.

The movie industry was getting into its stride to add to all the frivolity.

Francis and Arabella were astonished at the sheer energy of their daughter and her friends. While their parents sipped champagne or wine or spirits, their young Charleston'd, Black Bottomed, and generally had the fun which they craved, fuelled by copious amounts of soft drinks. The jazz band was equally indefatigable. Fairhaven's ballroom had seen nothing like it – ever.

Neither was Arabella required to sing. How times had changed – irrevocably.

At midnight Cinderella was brought into the centre of a huge circle. They joined hands and advanced on her and then retired, faster and faster singing HAPPY BIRTHDAY followed by a very loud rendition of FOR SHE'S A JOLLY GOOD FELLOW.

As they broke up with shouts of laughter so at last did Amber's party, to be talked over for ages afterwards.

"Sure, has been the greatest ever," said Amber's current squeeze Westley, as he stole a sweet kiss. This followed by a less romantic "See ya" before they all swept off home.

Gosh soon it would be back to school.

For Francis, Amber's birthday marked his return to his role at Grantley's New York offices. It was intended to be a gradual re-introduction to his duties. However, the demands of his position were endless, and all too soon he was working all day, every day, Arabella and Dorothea protested when he intended to start going in on Saturday mornings and at least won that argument.

For Arabella, the change was startling. Instead of Francis's care being the centre of her life she was left to her own devices. She felt rather aimless after a time. The usual longing for Courtneys began to develop. Even the renewal of her bond with Amber could not stifle it.

Hugh Davenport, the impresario who had discovered her and managed her career, had approached her with the idea for her to star in a new Broadway show. Though tempted, Arabella felt drained after nursing Francis and gently rejected the part, but not the idea of a future return to the stage.

One Sunday as Amber and her mother walked in the garden, they both flinched as a giant grey bird swooped over them with a whoosh of air, and the sound of a very noisy engine.

They saw a figure in a leather helmet and goggles leaning from the cockpit and waving to them.

"It must be Annette trying out her latest plane!" exclaimed Arabella.

"Wow! and Wow!" cried her daughter.

"To be able to soar like a giant bird but with no wings flapping. To be able to reach into the heavens and with all below just dots. I ADORE it. Aunt Netty will surely teach me to fly."

There could never ever be an alternative.

CHAPTER 12
<u>AMBER</u> – Into the clouds

Amber had made her decision and while she lived nothing would ever change it. She would learn to fly – to soar like the birds which thronged America, but with no feathers, all her food would be of the spirit. A plane would need to be strong and gallant, and she would care for it as she had for Wing and Cedric.

Soon her room was littered with aircraft magazines, her heroes were the air aces who had flown during the war. She drew pictures of their planes endlessly and labelled every part. She learned the function of every component. Now she must impress her Aunt and be able to transfer so many facts into action. When she reeled off so much information pointing to their whereabouts on a model which Francis had given her, Aunt Netty held up her hands in surrender. "O.K., O.K., I'll take you to the field on Saturday and introduce you to my best ground engineer. You need to know the inside of an engine and how it works. No, it's no good pleading you have so much to learn before I take you up. Perhaps on your next birthday."

Ambrose White had never had such a diligent and inquisitive pupil, nor one so young. She was a Grantley through and through, curious, determined, ready to question something she disagreed with, and with a suggestion to improve the matter.

He reported to her aunt, "I can't believe she is so young, ma'am. She shows a maturity beyond her years. I am bombarded with questions, but they are never pointless. If her flying proves to be as good as her theoretical knowledge she'll be a sensational pilot."

'Mmm' replied her aunt, "perhaps, we must wait and see. Also, she must complete her normal education."

"Hers is an enthusiasm which we must nurture and not quench. Do think on it ma'am. We've got the time now the war is over."

The war was indeed over, but the exploits of the wartime pilots so stirringly reported in American newspapers had released a tide of interest in flying. Americans were rich enough to gain their licences and buy their own planes and many intrepidly competed in flying contests. Soon there would be flying circuses and the fragile boxlike early aircrafts, rapidly developed into more sturdy planes. War certainly results in very swift changes.

Amber's notebooks featured on the left-hand page's photographs of aeroplanes, and on the right-hand side her sketches, annotations and questions. Three wings had given way to two, with much more powerful engines. Soon she was convinced all would be single winged.

Now she persuaded her Aunt to take her to the Grantley

design offices, and onto the factory floor. Her Aunty Netty was torn between the knowledge that Amber was the only Grantley heir, and needed all the information she so craved, and the need to safeguard her adventurous niece.

The exploits of the Lafayette Squadron were legion. Several American airmen under French leadership had volunteered to fight in 1915. They had named their squadron after the famous Frenchman Gilbot De Motier, Marquis de Lafayette, who had fought in the American Civil War. His name was synonymous with courage and valour, against overwhelming odds.

The Yankee pilots, seven at first, were repaying America's debt, because it was the right thing to do. Soon others joined them.

Amber knew every bit of their history, and when an ex 'Lafayette' was giving a talk in New York, she was determined to be there.

Seated with her Aunts and Uncles in the best seats, she was spellbound.

Her hand shot up and her question regarding the relative firepower of German compared to French planes, was courteously answered.

"I'll do it. I'll fly and I'll fight in a war, just see if I don't. I'll be a Lafayette too.," she muttered.

Aunt Netty was so impressed by her well-informed Niece that she allowed her to go up with one of the outfits giving flights at an airshow. She reasoned that as they did it day in and day out for a living, they must be highly experienced and with well-maintained planes. That reasoning deserted her as she watched the plane take off and complete its circuits. Despite it landing safely she determined that in future she and only she would be responsible for Amber's tuition and safety.

Amber returned in a rush of excitement and stated again that she must become a pilot. Ever aware, she had realised that if the plane was too far from its home field, she must study navigation too.

Annette remembered her own conversion to flying and recognised that this was a fire not to be extinguished, Netty had decided the time had come.

"I am going to provide you with your own training plane. No-one else will fly it except my deputy and myself. It will be kept in a secure hangar."

"The day you can escort me to the plane, explain how its engine works, together with the controls and safety checks, then and only then will we go up."

Two months short of her next birthday the task was completed to Annette's satisfaction, the plane was fuelled and ready.

"There is one further thing you must always do, that is a visual check of your plane. It must become a habit as natural to you as breathing."

"What am I looking for Aunt Netty?"

"Anything that doesn't look right or feel right, you'll just know."

This done, at last, the two-seater trainer took off. Amber's sensations were even more wonderful than on her first short spin. Now her aunt shared with her every aspect of the plane's capabilities, short of aerobatics.

The sky reached out to her, the very few clouds sported with her, the sun shone and the feeling of weightlessness which allowed her to soar above the mundane land below captivated Amber.

She watched the controls, felt the trim and balance and power, thought how the stick and rudder would feel when she was flying the ship. At last, she knew what it meant to feel the plane. Was that an odd vibration which needed checking? Did the craft veer to the starboard side a little? When they landed, she felt dizzy with happiness.

"You must keep a log, Amber. I want you to record date/type of plane/number of hours/weather conditions and any problems."

"It may be repetitive as you are flying as a passenger/pupil, but it will be a valuable record for you."

This done Aunt and Niece began the drive back to Fairhaven for a well-deserved dinner.

Regular reports had kept Arabella in touch with both Maggie Jones, her house manager, and John Jarvis, her estate manager. Both were long serving and utterly reliable.

The telegraph from Maggie caught Arabella unprepared.

"Must leave Courtneys at once. Will explain in person when possible. Can you return or shall we close the house? Apologetically Maggie."

Either Courtneys, Grantley's or her earlier career were always interrupting her marriage. When she shared the news with Francis, Amber and Dorothea, they all knew that she must go to England to sort out her staffing changes. The immediacy of Maggie's telegraph would not allow an orderly changeover there.

Amber just rolled her eyes and prepared to bid adieu once more to her mother. The pendulum had swung again as Dorothea waved her daughter-in-law off from Fairhaven. An anguished Francis did the same from the quayside in New York, as his wife, lover, nurse and saviour sailed away. Neither could be vanquished the thought that he might never see her again.

The summer of her 16th birthday saw Amber flying solo

OFFICIALLY. Her log altered to solo, and her trusty Harvard trainer was exchanged for a Grantley.

Now she could log up hours and hours until she was old enough to gain her private pilot's licence aged 17.

Now she must become so accomplished that no-one could forbid her all the opportunities that flying offered. The old wooden-framed linen-covered planes had given way to the metal framed and covered, which could take larger more powerful engines and cover longer distances. She was sure that they would carry many passengers, freight and mail commercially. It was a heady future.

With her pilot's licence, she would enter lots of air races and become jolly famous.

'You see if I don't.'

Thankfully, she had the good sense to keep those ambitions to herself – except of course for Ambrose White, her ground engineer and tutor.

"You'll go far Miss Amber, but just wait until the right plane comes along. With that and your licence they'll be no holding you." 'Thanks Whitey,' she grinned "we'll conquer the world, won't we?"

He gave her a thumbs up and went off shaking his head at her sheer determination. She could already outfly her Aunt, and every other student or pilot at the Grantley airfield. Her flying was intuitive, but always based on her plane, weather conditions and the occasion. She wanted to fly to their other fields, especially in California, where their new aircraft designs were produced and tested. There she could watch the company test pilots flying the planes across the skies and checking, checking, checking for likely faults and necessary adaption.

"I can do that, I know I can, I'll be a test pilot too, even if I have to wait until I own Grantley Aircraft Company."

Amber wrote of her ambitions and progress to her still absent mother. The sky was her metier and would be her and the company's future. Arabella never doubted her bold daughter's future success. She would become a great aviatrix, for the world would indeed become her oyster.

The great Curtiss aircraft company out of New York was the most famous American company, with a huge reputation for their planes' success in winning air races and carrying mail. Amber could not be disloyal to her family business, but longed to fly a Curtiss plane, and vowed that when she was 17, she would do so, even using an assumed name. Plans were forever formulating in her active mind.

She regarded the frivolous lifestyles of her friends' older brothers and sisters with disdain. For her nothing beat the thrill of speed, for them fun, fun and more fun was the order of the day and especially of the night. Nightclubs and speakeasies did roaring business in every great city. Their bright young clientele had money and knew how to spend it. Excess became normal as the decade sped by.

Prohibition had resulted in all out war between the police and racketeers who used a hundred ingenious ways to provide booze for the eager customers. Their violent encounters were to spawn a whole new era of movies when Edward G Robinson would become public enemy number 1.

CHAPTER 13
ARABELLA – Return to her first love

Arabella's return to Courtneys was full of anxiety as to what she would find awaiting her. The joy of seeing her beloved home never failed to uplift and nurture her, but she couldn't help noticing that all was not as pristine as on her departure. The gravel drive needed raking, and some weeds were evident amongst the stones. The brass door knocker and bell pull, which usually shone so brightly, were dull and in need of some elbow grease.

Maggie had done her best with the staff available to her, but as her condition developed, she'd become rather overwhelmed. When Arabella saw her house manager the problem was obvious.

"Oh Maggie, do come and sit down while I order us some tea."

The lady in question was only too eager to do so and began her story at once.

"While you were away in America during the war, I fell in love for the first time in my life with one of the patients here. I think it happened over drinks and laughter in Finch's botty with the other chaps. When the war ended and the officers returned home, John wrote to me from Yorkshire and asked me to marry him. I had accepted, and agreed that once you settled back in, I would help you find new staff, and then we would marry. This took longer to do that I expected, and once you were nursing Mr Francis, I could not desert you, and John agreed to a further delay. We met when we could, 'DO you remember the night you invited me to supper at the Dower House? That was one evening when he was here, I worried that he would lose patience with me, but he is a good kind man. During your time back in America we married quietly, and he has a job here. I never dreamed I could become pregnant at my age. We are both delighted, but he does want to settle back in Yorkshire near to his family. I'm 6 months on and dare not wait any longer, hence my telegram full of urgency. I'll be leaving you short of staff and with no one in charge of the house for you. I couldn't be more sorry or upset."

"Dear Maggie" said Arabella taking her hands "You have given up so very, very much for me, and seen me through so many upsets. Now you must think of your husband and your baby. It is such a marvellous surprise. You must have time to rest and enjoy the precious months together. Of course, I understand and am so completely thankful to you for everything you have done here. Courtneys has been your home too, and a happy one, I hope. I haven't told Francis yet, but I realise I can't return to America. Here I belong, and it is due to you and Finch and cook and everyone who has worked so hard that this glorious house still loves and protects us all. I just so fondly hope that your new home will bring you so much joy."

With that they hugged each other, and Maggie burst into tears of relief.

"I'll bring John in to meet you tomorrow, and will leave on Friday, your room is all ready and cook will serve supper. Will you excuse me now I am just a little overtired?"

Arabella sank into her chair and drank a cup of the cold tea which she had left untouched. She realised that her admission to Maggie of her intention to remain at Courtneys, had been simmering in her head. Once she had spoken the words there could be no going back.

John was all that Maggie had promised when she introduced him to Arabella on the following morning. He spoke quietly, with none of the bluster associated with some ex-army officers, and his love for his pregnant wife was clear.

When they left her, it was agreed that Arabella would advertise in the local and national press for Maggie's replacement. A new head gardener and two more maids would also be needed. She hoped that these could be recruited locally, for part-time work and the option to 'live-out' were now the order of the day.

She realised that by referring to her late mother's records as housekeeper at Courtneys, she would find much valuable information and advice.

Note to Self

The funding depends on Francis's continued support. If this stalls be prepared to return to singing!!!

Oh no – surely not. Nearing 50 the music of the jazz age was not for her. Neither was her voice up to recitals, despite her daily vocal exercises. As she stood uncertainly in the library she remembered her mother's brisk tone.

"Don't just think about it, get on with it. Action will help you see the way ahead."

So instead of sitting down with a book, Arabella, to cook's astonishment, collected a cleaning basket, checked its contents, and with rolled up sleeves and apron in place set to and shone up all the brass on the front door.

Day by day her energy, which had been sapped by Francis's long illness was restored. Arabella started each day early as she had done as a lowly housemaid.

As she sat in the peace of her home the silence rebuked her. It should have been alive with the sounds of children. At least three of her own should have grown up there. Their families should now be running along the corridors and playing in the garden.

Now the silent nursery and staff room corridors and bedrooms she had so carefully refurbished were just redundant.

It was small comfort that so many neighbouring estates were in the same situation. Courtneys was her responsibility, and she must keep it alive and thriving for her grandchildren yet to be born.

The applications for the post advertised began to arrive.

Only one applicant seemed suitable. It was a Mrs McGuire returning to England after some years in Ireland. Arabella wrote at once to arrange an interview as there was no telephone number. She sent polite letters to inform the other hopefuls that the post had been filled.

When Mrs McGuire presented herself, neat and pretty, and roughly Arabella's age, Arrabella could not believe her eyes. There before her stood Bridie who had served her for so long as dresser, then in charge of the house until her marriage to the local doctor. Bridie had enlivened many a day as they toured America while Arabella established her career. Back at Courtneys, with her younger sister taking on the role of Arabella's dresser, she had proved her worth, beguiling all who came into contact with her. Why had her name changed from that of her doctor husband Daniels to McGuire?

"Sure, it was the fortunes of war Miss Arabella. For me misfortunes! The doctor was killed in France in 1916, and I was still left looking after any old locum doctor at the surgery. Eddy was 8 and a real handful. I've always been unlucky in my men, and Michael McGuire fitted the bill fine. Before I knew it, I'd sold the house to the latest locum and me, and Eddy were back to Ireland. The nightgown was lifted as quick as me savings, and he was off. Thankfully, Doctor Daniels had left a trust fund for Eddy's schooling. I sent him off to boarding school and have worked ever since. When I saw your advertisement, I cried for joy, so I did. Will I come back to help you? Will yous be staying in England for long? Are yous due back to America? How're Mr Francis and Miss Amber doing?"

Arabella laughed and held up her hands in submission.

"Slow down Bridie. I am trying to take in your latest adventure.

Yes, of course you've got your old job back.

Yes, I intend to stay in England.

No, I have no plans to go back to America.

Mr Francis is much better, and Miss Amber is too busy with her flying to miss me a jot. She'll be the American Amy Johnson without a doubt."

"Well, isn't that all grand," said Bridie.

"When will I start, and do you need any of me relatives over to help like the Irish boys did before that rotten war? Did you know Paddy and Liam were both killed so they were? Micky only missed the recruitment cos his leg was broke when the mare he was mating with Raven kicked out with the thrill of it all."

They couldn't help laughing in their old companiable way. They looked around the house and gardens together. Bridie accepted her new wages, and both agreed it would be better for her to use a bedroom on the guest corridor, so Arabella was not alone in the house at night.

"I'll serve me notice and be back after a week. Will I write to me Cousin Angus O'Neill – he's half Scottish and'll be brilliant in the garden? At least he don't sing like the old Finch did, nor get drunk as far as I know?"

"Yes, do that please Bridie, and I'll wait for you to interview for new maids as you'll be working with them."

Bridie was humming merrily to herself as she set off for the station, and Arabella with the help of Edie began to 'turn out' Bridie's room. Life was going to be so much brighter now.

If her daughter could drive at such an early age surely Arabella could learn to drive? She would ask Christopher Richards to teach her.

Steve Maitland had taken over as estates manager after John Jarvis's retirement. Their meeting had not been reassuring. The farms' profits were falling as crops brought in less money. He had managed to increase yields but was anxious about the future.

These were not easy times.

Arabella reflected that Francis's declaration after his return from captivity had moved her greatly. It was by relying on the images of her stage performances and the thrilling music which had kept him alive. Yet despite their constant nearness as he recovered, they had been unable to resume their previous easy intimacy, and it hurt both of them deeply.

If the income from Courtneys estate was to fall off, she would be even more reliant on the allowances from Francis. These had continued with utter reliability from his London office throughout their marriage. Suppose he lost patience with her and discontinued them. Where would that leave her? 'What if,' and 'if only,' buttered no parsnips. It was action which saved the day. Time to contact her London agent and scan The Stage Magazine.

Arabella had regained her enviable figure by so much

physical hard work. Properly presented, it would, like her voice, serve her well.

She would soon discover there was a new medium which did not require her to be seen by her audience.

CHAPTER 14

AMBER – In Full Flight

Amber's 17th birthday seemed to have taken years to arrive! At last, there was something in her life that she couldn't stamp her foot for and be given it at once. Her privileged life was just normal to her, as all her friends led similar ones.

She had opened her birthday gifts with much gratitude. Not so much for the gifts themselves, though they were certainly grand and very expensive. It was the occasion they marked which caused her to sparkle with excitement. The one from England, accompanied a most unsuitable card of a painting of roses. It was the gift from her mother which was so special. Somehow, she had obtained the wartime flying log recovered from a dead Lafayette pilot's body. It was not macabre, just a magnificent tribute to a brave and special pilot. Amber couldn't wait to ring Arabella and thank her 'enormously,' assuring her that she would treasure it forever.

Her own logbooks were now so extensive, recording flight after flight, as her aunt had instructed. Now at long last she could apply for her longed for Pilot Licence (USA), issued by the Aeronautical Association of the USA. Soon she would hold the 3" x 4" leather bound booklet with four pages, including a photograph of the aviator, plus signature. The printed request to aid and assist the holder of the certificate was written in English, plus French, German, Italian, Spanish and Greek.

After breakfast her father, aunts and uncles all drove out to the airfield. Dorothea, feeling a little afraid, watched from a parked car.

Ambrose White, Amber's ground engineer, gave her a smart salute before swinging open the hangar doors. There, decorated with blue balloons, stood the family's gift to her. She ran towards it with arms outstretched. The plane was a single seater model in silver livery. Aunt Netty had developed it in partnership with Lockheed to produce a sleek, reliable, fast craft, which could take on all comers at the many air shows and races. Once she had become accustomed to it, Amber could now do what she had been born for.

"I ADORE it, and I ADORE you all for giving me my heart's desire." With that she flung her arms around each of them in turn for a hug and kisses.

"Don't think you are going up until you've learned all the controls," said Netty.

"No Aunt" she said dutifully and began the task at once.

When they had all gone on their various ways, she asked Ambrose why Grantley's was collaborating with Lockheed. "It's the competition Miss Amber, there are too many firms producing planes, and the market is slowing. Your Aunt Phillipa is finding it the same with her cars."

Some firms will fail, and some survive by joining forces. Amber was thoughtful as she sat in the cockpit of her wondrous new plane. Could it really be true? Were the good times about to end? Surely America was so wealthy that nothing could slow her progress?

Quickly she cast the thoughts aside, concentrated on the

task in hand, and began to plan her first long distance flight from East to West Coast. She intended to start from New York and fly to Burbank in California. Her aunt might believe that the Grantley plant there was her interest, but Amber had another. The movie sets would be her targets.

For such a long flight she needed Ambrose White with all his experience as her flight engineer. He would ensure that all was well before preceding her to the first re-fuelling stop. He would make a full check before her final leg into Los Angeles. Amber had determined that she would fly 'non-stop' with no overnight or rest breaks, just quick re-fuelling and safety checks. Too many small producers and airlines were failing or amalgamating with other manufacturers and airlines. Even the famous Glenn Curtiss had joined up with the Wright Brothers.

If Amber could keep the name of Grantley's ever before the public, and make it seem extra glamorous and desirable, then their planes would sell.

The great day arrived with all the newspapers having been assured of a scoop. The publicity for her epic flight was phenomenal. As she posed beside Silver Arrow the press photographers were fighting for position. Climbing into the cockpit Amber gave them a cheery wave. Her ground crew all wore silver overalls with a flying arrow on the back. Amber took flight with a crescendo of noise dipped her wings in salute and was soon out of sight.

The headlines screamed 'Silver Arrow sets off for L.A. with its 17-year-old pilot, or 'Golden Grantley Girl set for Glory – 18-hour flight ahead'.

The copywriters had let their imagination take flight, too much was made of Amber's experience, confidence and beauty. Too much for male fliers to compete with.

Her reception in L.A. was even more rapturous less than 18 hours later, flasks of hot coffee, ham sandwiches and hard-boiled eggs having sustained her throughout the flight. Close attention to the compass, favourable winds and a steady fuel conserving speed had served her well. '17-year-old Grantley Heiress lands safely. She looked as fresh as paint when she jumped down from her plane, waved to the crowd and blew kisses. What a trouper. What an aviatrix,' Amber blessed the lipstick and rouge which had given her colour and sparkle.

She slept and relaxed for several days, conducted her interviews and allowed the fanfare to die down. The passengers boarding the bus for a tour of Hollywood studios were the usual mixed bunch. No one remarked on the young woman wearing a cool summer dress and sheltering under a large sun hat. Her vivid eyes were hidden behind large dark shades.

As she returned to the bus between each of the many studios, she appeared to be keeping a record of them. Sam Goldwyn, Adolph Zucker, Louis B Mayer, Warner Brothers, all headed up major studios and were household names, just like the new stars they created. Who would ever forget Al Jolson in the Jazz Singer? Then there were the glamorous women, who every woman wanted to emulate, and to swoon over Valentino.

It was a much smaller studio which saw the biggest entry in the young woman's notebook.

Its two directors Sammy Lewis and Jason Russell were puzzled to receive a letter from Julius Cartwright, it stated that he had a proposition for them which would be to their advantage, both financially and artistically. Since he was a very respected lawyer and featured the word finance, a meeting was quickly agreed.

Julius Cartwright arrived at their office on Lot 4 with two secretaries, so he surely meant business. The younger one looked somehow familiar to Sammy. She wore a smart summer linen dress, little makeup and hair in a tight French pleat.

Following brisk handshakes and introductions, Julius Cartwright got down to business.

"I am directed to enquire if your studio has the facilities and expertise to produce an aviation movie. It need not be long or have a large cast. There would be ground staff I presume, but the main aim is to record the aerial exploits of the pilot. Lots of aerobatics, and most of all to evoke the feeling of speed. I presume you'll be able to hire great cameramen and great pilots to safely record our principal."

"If you can provide an estimate of the costs we would make a very substantial contribution. If you can assure us of widespread distribution, and if all this can be achieved within the shortest possible time, my principal is willing to re-invest profits into your business. There are indications that America is on the verge of economic problems. Should you be able to carry off this film it would increase your chances of survival. Any questions?"

"You bet," the young men said in unison.

"First who's the pilot we'll be featuring?"

"That'll be me" said the younger woman shaking out her hair, and assuming a far more confident manner. "I'm Amber Grantley," she coolly informed them as she shook hands.

"Gosh – the Grantley trust babe" burst out Sammy. "I thought I recognised you."

"May we congratulate you on your epic flight," said Jason, the more thoughtful of the pair of young executives.

"Thank you" replied Amber quietly "May we sit and discuss the matter to hammer out what we each expect. Then we can leave you to let us know your answer. I shall be extremely busy flying, so if we are to do it, we need to know how long you will need me for. I realise that we must be technically perfect, there are far too many careless deaths."

Sooner than any of them could have expected, the Wall Street crash would result in many suicides, as men realised that they faced total ruin. Fortunes were wiped out in a flash as the whole of America and then the world, realised that everything was overvalued or over ambitious or unsustainable. Where America led, the knock-on effects ensued that the world would follow. The rich became suddenly poor, and the very poor became destitute. They needed escapist entertainment to help them to forget their troubles for a few short hours.

The movies were the perfect answer. They offered double-bill showings and cheap tickets. The producers used more stage actors, providing natural acting in believable plots, ideal for a subdued and worried population. The movie

87

industry was – against all odds – thriving and expanding. One of its most popular offerings was of a young airwoman.

'The adventures of 'Aviatrix Amber,' caused audiences to gasp with astonishment at the exploits of the young airwoman who could fling her silver plane across the skies. At one moment she would be climbing almost vertically, then plunging in a steep dive. She flew upside down, in spirals, in loops and head on until the last possible second.

Amber was soon famous, her studio financially secure, and her many record- breaking flights always news. All of which reflected well on Grantley Aeronautics.

CHAPTER 15
FRANCIS – Dilemmas and Changes

With production cut back in all areas, Francis had faced what became known as the Great Depression, using the strategy which Randolph would have adopted. It grieved him to lay off so many of their loyal and skilled workforce. The board of directors had decided to give them 20% pay until business recovered enough to re-employ them. If they could get another job in the meantime, it was all to the good.

His approach made Francis headlines as 'The Caring Industrialist.'

His fearless daughter continued to break some records and to establish new ones for new routes. American aviation which had been encouraged by the POSTMASTER GENERAL to distribute the mail across America, then worldwide, was enviable and led the world.

As his country faced long years of depression, so Francis took the decision to end his long years without Arabella. He still spoke to her regularly by transatlantic telephone. Now at last he asked her formally to return to him and their marriage in America. There was a lengthy silence. Surely, she must have anticipated that after so many years apart their present situation could not continue.

He closed his eyes and visualised her sitting in the library, which he had refurbished for her at Courtneys. When she spoke, her voice was tremulous, so unlike her unusual strong sweet tones. "I have been expecting this Francis, and I do see that you need me there as your wife, or to be free of me.

I've loved you deeply, but our lives are too separate, and now we are older, it is too difficult to bridge the gap. You have been so kind and generous to me in every way, and I thank you for all the great moments we shared. Do give my love to Dorothea and our dear daughter. Goodbye."

"'Goodbye Arabella' he responded, I'll be contacting you via our lawyers very soon."

What she had feared had come to pass. Francis had not mentioned finances, so she must await his offer. If she had to give up Courtneys, it would break her heart. Yet moving back to America would be even worse. She supposed that she could make the dower house her home. Yet she felt far too young, there was ambition and talent and her beauty to sustain her.

She picked up the telephone and asked to be connected to her London agent.

It would be soon enough to share the news with Bridie when the letter arrived. Arabella opened the letter with foreboding, she would go up to London to discuss its contents with her lawyer. She had retained the same firm which Hugh Davenport had engaged for her when she had first set out on her career aged 19. Now, years later, she must consult with the new senior partners on matters which would surely affect the rest of her life.

The letter's contents were completely terse and business like.

Mr Francis Grantley would petition for divorce on the grounds on constructive desertion by Mrs Arabella Grantley, which had continued for some years.

He was willing to continue her personal allowance for the future. However, the annual allowance to maintain her house and estate at Courtneys could not continue at its present level. As a gesture of goodwill, he was willing to pay it at a level of 80% for five years to allow her to re-order her life. This would then be subject to an offer after that date. He would continue to totally support the only child of their union, Miss Amber Grantley, until she reached her 21st birthday. Amber was free at any time to visit her mother with no constraints. Each of them were free to reclaim any personal items left at each other's homes.

Each were free to marry in the future with no changes to these provisions.

The letter ended with Mr Grantley wishing his (soon to be former) wife Arabella Grantley good health and good fortune in the years ahead.

Francis's generosity and good wishes quite undid Arabella, and she wept unashamedly.

"Come come Mrs Grantley. It is sad that your marriage has come to an end. However, I have never been faced with such a generous settlement offer, I urge you to take it at once."

"Oh, I know, Mr Burdett, but I am at fault for my marriage breakdown. It is so very typical of Francis to be so generous and forgiving."

"It may comfort you to know that in a letter to me explaining his motives, he attributes to your care and determination the fact that he recovered so well from his wartime incarceration.

Without you, the fortunes of Grantley corporation might not have flourished."

"Thank you," Arabella replied, "please inform my husband that I will accept his terms and that I am grateful to him."

They shook hands, and as she left Mr Burdett could well understand the allure which had kept Mr Grantley enthralled for these many absent years.

He sighed and called for his secretary to take down his client's response and despatch it to America.

Arabella's second call was unexpectedly fruitful. Clive Peacock had bought the agency from Hugh Davenport and with his predecessor's good name and client list had expanded it greatly. He lacked the courtly presence of his handsome predecessor, but made up for it with huge confidence, enthusiasm, and wit. Arabella thought he might have done well on the music halls himself.

"Sit down, sit down dear lady" he insisted. "How splendid to meet you at last. I have not been idle and let me say many people are thrilled at the prospect of hearing your glorious voice again." Accepting his compliment, Arabella looked at him enquiringly.

"I have an offer for you to have your own programme on the wireless. It will be for 30 minutes and the producer, he's been promised a prime time at 8pm. To publicise it they want people to write in with their favourite song. Instead of it just being announced, you will introduce each song. Also, if the listener would like it dedicated to a loved one, you can do that too. It may take up time, but the idea is that the listeners will feel personally involved. What do you think?

Do you want to give it a try?"

Arabella quite liked the novelty of the new format. It might leave her open to some songs which would not suit her range. If there were enough letters there would surely be the basis for her programmes. Also, she would sing her own choices and introduce songs which might be new to the listeners. It would pay to be adaptable. "How many weeks would they like me to sing for? Shall I be able to rehearse beforehand? Shall I have a pianist or a small orchestra? Shall I have a break for a solo instrumentalist during the half hour?"

Mr Peacock was scribbling furiously and knew there would be many more questions. His client was a great performer and knew the pitfalls of live stage performances. It was obvious that she knew nothing of recorded programmes, which could be edited or re-recorded before transmission.

Arabella was astonished at the fees she was to receive, and her agent assured her that if the listening figures were high, she could expect even more for a second series. Despite her long absence from the stage, she was still venerated by many who had attended her concerts.

Clive Peacock astonished her even more by expecting there would be scope to sell gramophone records too.

A second career beckoned, and Arabella would do her very best to ensure that it was as successful as her first. It would be stimulating to be back in the public eye and besides, she needed the money. But not as urgently as she might have, because Francis's offer of settlement was so very generous.

Soon both she and Francis were indeed in the public eye via

the gossip columns popular in both countries. The references were thinly veiled and let to speculation of their domestic arrangements.

"Which wealthy industrialist has begun steps to end his marriage to a world-famous singer, who forged her career here in America?" was a prime example.

In England, the emphasis was reversed, though the message was the same.

"Which singing star, who has lived apart from her wealthy American husband, will launch a wireless programme? We hear that divorce proceedings will soon follow their long separation."

Both were mortified, but Clive Peacock regarded all the speculative publicity as invaluable, and so it proved. At least their facts were accurate. The American film gossips would happily ruin lives and careers to obtain a scoop, fictitious or not.

Arabella's producer had decided that her programmes should go out 'live.' Because of her experience, she was unlikely to dry up, although he had someone on hand to intervene should she be overcome by nerves.

They both felt that the immediacy of speaking live to her audience, then singing 'their song' would work well.

The letters poured in, often with touching messages for a loved one, or in memory of one lost to them.

Rehearsals were constantly interrupted to change an arrangement or alter a phrase or emphasis.

Arabella found it both annoying and stimulating. As a professional singer she was used to taking the stage and having ironed out all problems beforehand, then to give a perfect performance. Here changes could be made at the last minute and had to be taken in her stride.

She spoke through the large cumbersome microphone but envisioned the person she was speaking to. She smiled, looked sad and changed her tone according to the requirements of the message. With that, her warmth and sincerity made contact with her listeners before she paused, adjusted her breathing and began to sing.

Her Aunt Alice, who had been a theatre dresser before accompanying Arabella on tour, had insisted that no costume should restrict her breathing, but must always be both elegant and comfortable. Arabella, with the help of Bridie, embraced this view. Her costumes may be simpler, but as she would be photographed frequently, also smart.

Some wireless performers were more careless in their dress as they were unseen by their audiences. Not so Arabella – besides if she looked good then she would feel good, and her performance would be enhanced.

Arabella gave a sigh of relief as the red light winked off after her final "goodnight and sweet dreams."

Her producer, Alexander Ross, congratulated her. "Can we meet up on Tuesday for a review and to confirm all the items before your next rehearsal? I'll have some feedback and listening figures for you then."

Bridie had travelled from Courtneys with her earlier in the day. They returned to their hotel, shared a supper with Clive

Peacock, who was full of his usual enthusiasms, then fell into bed.

So, Arabella's new career was established.

She found it far less demanding than her operas and recitals. Popular music was easier to sing but required ceaseless sincerity or it became hackneyed. It was as well that her first series was almost at an end. She was due to start a second in the Autumn. Summer at Courtneys beckoned. There would be the usual deliberation with her estate manager, and a formal meeting with Bridie regarding the house. Still, she would enjoy the golden days and the roses. When they returned to Courtneys, two surprise letters sat on her desk.

The first was enclosed with a covering letter from Francis's London office. Guy Winterton had received it with other mail but marked for his attention only. It was to be forwarded to Arabella from him.

Francis wrote –

"Dear Arabella,

I have to warn you that some unfortunate gossip is about to break, which will inevitably involve you. My lawyers assure me that it will not affect our divorce. The decree absolute is to be granted any day now.

The gossip and inuendo links me to my secretary, Miss Lucinda Atcheson. Miss Atcheson has been in the post for three years now. She is of unimpeachable reputation and from a fine family. Owing to the depression, she needed to take up employment and obtained a post with Grantley's. I have come to admire her quiet efficiency and character. She reminds me greatly of my mother in those respects. Dorothea has in fact met her at a reception at Fairhaven. It was she who pointed out the regard I had for Lucinda and where it might lead in the future.

My new attachment in no way reduces my gratitude to you for the happy years we spent together. You are the mother of our beloved girl. You know how gossip can reduce real affection to a squalid level. We must not let it happen to us, I ask you to be aware and to deal with newspapers in your usual charming manner.

  Yours, Francis"

Arabella's astonishment was only tempered by her curiosity. Who on earth was Lucinda Atcheson? How old was she and what did she look like? She certainly was a paragon of virtue but had managed to capture Francis's heart and caused him to break out of the pretence of his long-distance marriage. Arabella knew by his courtly language that he had indeed fallen in love and would surely marry after a suitable interval. Whilst she wished him nothing but happiness, she felt wistful after so many years as his wife.

Her cable to him was terse. Almost military. Received and understood. Please inform Amber,

  Yours, A

Arabella rarely drank, apart from a celebratory glass of champagne. Now she moved onto the drinks tray and mixed herself a whisky and water. Some unknown urge caused her to raise her glass to Sir Edward and Sir Charles Courtney. They had both influenced her greatly, changing her life completely. Now she must face new challenges and do it with grit and flair if Courtneys was to prosper and not merely survive. Courtneys, always Courtneys. It had outlasted her marriage, the years she had spent apart from her daughter and still she loved it with a depth she found unfathomable. So be it!

Francis's warning was timely and the respite brief. The telephone calls from London newspapers were intrusive and persistent. After fielding the early calls herself, Arabella left it to Bridie or one of the maids. There replies were all standard.

"Thank you so much for your call and interest, Mrs Grantley has no comment at this time."

With this standard reply, interest soon fell away – that is until Arabella received a letter from a New York firm of lawyers. She read with incredulity and mounting anger.

Dear Mrs Grantley,

Further to reports of your husband's affair with another woman, we would like to offer our services to you. You should be able to set aside your present divorce proceedings and petition him for his adultery to be recognised. This would result in a far greater settlement for you. Our terms for acting would be reasonably set at 10% of the settlement sum.

Yours etc

Pierce & Barrett (Attorneys)

'How dare they' thought Arabella.

How despicable and how could they know of her present

settlement details?

She immediately sent it to Stephen Burdett with the request that a copy be urgently sent round to Guy Winterton at Grantley's offices!

It was an affront to Francis and Mrs Atcheson. Could the Grantley company lawyers take on these opportunist people? Surely, they were guilty of libel at the very least, plus defamation of character?!

Her next action was to reassure her daughter.

Her parents' marriage might be nearing its end but the love for Amber would always be showed and put to her care and best interests. Neither held any animosity towards the other, only deep respect and affection.

The letter included her latest photograph taken on the steps of Courtneys. Arabella fondly hoped that regular photographs, in some way kept her alive in her daughter's memory.

CHAPTER 16
AMBER – The way ahead

Amber was now almost twenty and was cutting a swathe through the aviation world. No record was safe from her. No route too difficult for her to pioneer and establish.

She did indeed fly Curtiss planes and those of all the great American manufacturers.
Even her Aunt Netty authorised her to fly the Grantley planes in early production. She was aware that her brilliant niece would pick up any shortcomings and help in the development of a better craft. In effect, she was a company test pilot.

Amber had found time to enjoy some of the fun-packed times of the 1920s. She loved to dance to the lively jazz tunes but absolutely refused any form of liquor. She was too young, and alcohol would affect her judgement while flying. Nothing and no one could compete with planes, so boys soon gave up on her despite her good looks and desirable wealth.

These heady times had given way to the more sombre 30s when money and jobs were scarce. It was thanks to her exploits the Grantley Aeronautics could continue, collaborating but was not swallowed up.

Now her world was to be altered forever. It had been bad enough when Grandpa Randolph that great rumbustious man had died. She had quietly missed him so much.

Now her parents' marriage was to end in divorce like so many of her friends' families. O.K., her mother might have needed to live in England, Amber still remembered the 'golden lady' caught in the spotlights of the New York theatre and reaching out to her daughter with that thrilling voice of hers. Why, oh why, hadn't they met for so long? Amber was perfectly capable of flying over to England.

It was 1913 when she had left her English home so why had she dodged returning? Always, always too busy.

She now spoke to her mother on the transatlantic line, less often. It was too painful, but each made a solemn promise to the other that they would meet for Amber's 21st birthday in the summer of 1933.

Soon Amber, America and the entire world would once again be embroiled in turmoil and change.

CHAPTER 17
UPHEAVAL AND CHANGE

The weary 'Depression' wore on. People were poorer, unemployed, desperate even, but still the world lurched on. How quickly the Roaring 20's had given way to the despairing 30's.

A new politician with new ideas to lift America out of the doldrums was about to emerge. Franklin D. Roosevelt was neither a great orator nor a powerful personality, yet he was at once totally determined to rescue his country and his fellow Americans.

Money must be raised to pour into farming, building roads, bridges and dams, giving men and their families jobs and education and better lives.

Slowly people began to listen, and to believe that it might be possible, and oh so slowly it would be so.

Francis had other worries. The news coming out of Germany of the new fanatical Chancellor was so familiar to him. He observed had Germany's preparation for the 1914-18 war at first hand. Now he saw all these signs repeated and was convinced that a war was inevitable.

His contacts at the War Department were less convinced,

though they had noted that German mail planes looked remarkably like light bombers. Also, the sight of 24 Italian Flying boats in perfect formation enchanted Americans when they flew over New York.

Amber was in time to witness this display. Her interest in the Sneider Trophy International Air Race for seaplanes was tempered by the fact that flying boats had never appealed to her. No, they were too unwieldy, give her wheels and solid ground to take off and land anyday.

A certain New York legal practice, having been threatened by litigation, had speedily closed its doors and left the city.

Now that her father and mother were divorced, Amber realised that the break, however painful, was final and necessary.

Francis and Lucinda were married at a small ceremony, before both families. Their honeymoon destination was a close kept secret. It was all carefully timed to take place before Amber's 21st birthday celebrations in the Summer of 1933.

Dorothea had been totally supportive of her son's choice of a second wife. It had pained her to witness his loneliness. Fond as she was of Arabella, it was impossible to condone her desertion or wish it to continue.

Lucinda was quiet, confident and kind and would make a very suitable mistress of Fairhaven.

She contributed several useful ideas to the arrangements for her stepdaughters 21st birthday. It was to be a splendid affair designed to cast off depression blues. Young people would again take prominence, as for Ambers earlier birthday parties. The ballroom was to be decorated in silver and blue with models of Silver Arrow and other famous planes.

The band was one of the new 'Swing' Orchestras, and the caterers, newly freed from the bonds of prohibition, were well prepared for a bonanza event.

Amber had discovered that her old mantra – the only conversation worth having is about planes, no longer applied. She had met a young man who immediately attracted her. He had dark hair, dark soulful eyes and was given to quoting poetry.

At first, she had thought him 'soppy,' but soon amended that to soulful. Perhaps her hormones had been on hold, but when he kissed her WOW! It might not equal the thrill of flying, but it was pretty darn good. With David in mind, she chose an acceptable turquoise-blue gown for her party, rather than the startling scarlet she preferred.

The invitations had gone out a month before and were

eagerly accepted by their recipients.

Just one week before the great day Amber received an urgent cable from Bridie. Arabella had been admitted to a London hospital. She had been gravely ill, but was at last showing signs of recovery, alas not in time to be at Amber's 21st party!

Amber did what she always did in times of crisis. She ran to her grandmother's rooms. Dorothea would calm her and sooth her worries alright. Giving a brisk knock Amber entered, calling out for her grandmother.

"Granny, where are you? I've had horrid news. Mama is very ill and won't be at my party." Dorothea sat in her usual upright armchair. Her hands were folded neatly in her lap. She was absolutely still and quite dead.

Amber fell to her knees and took the cold hands into her young warm vibrant ones. There she stayed weeping tears of love and anguish for the woman who had poured so much devotion over her dearest girl ever since they had first touched hands when Amber was a baby. Amber knew in that instant that her life could never be the same. Yet she thought not of herself but of the great lady who had really acted as her mother for so many years. The whole family would be devastated without their matriarch.

It was Lucinda that found her and raised her to her feet and into her arms.

"Come my dear" she said, "we must tell the others so they can say goodbye. You must come with me now my dear."

"How strange," thought Amber, "she speaks and acts just like Dorothea," as she was led away holding a warm and comforting hand.

Francis informed the News Agencies, and their announcements were always respectful:

'The death of Dorothea Grantley, wife of the late Randolph Grantley of Grantley Industrial Corporation was announced today. Mrs Grantley was a notable hostess and patron of the arts. She was co-founder with her husband of the great art collection which is held at their family home Fairhaven in New York State. It comprises all the greatest paintings of the British portrait artists. Her unfailing support for many art projects will be sorely missed. She is survived by her three children, Mr Francis Grantley who heads the company, and his sisters. Mrs Phillipa Jameson runs the automobile section and Mrs Annette White in charge of aeronautics. Her only grandchild in the famous aviatrix Amber Grantley who will be 21 this weekend.

The tributes to Dorothea Grantley poured in. As a great American hostess, she had contributed to many institutions Art, Ballet, Opera, Theatre.

All acknowledged their debt to her for her support and encouragement.

Amber's 21st birthday invitations were replaced by Dorothea's funeral reception. The balloons were removed from the ballroom, but the aeroplane models remained, it was with his wife's constant support that Randolph had forged his great company. They had an abiding marriage and established the Grantley dynasty.

In her misery Amber turned to her beloved plane, took off and just flew and flew and flew. Even in the great sky she could not shake off her sorrow. What if Arabella died too? It was all too terrible.

Lucinda was the new rock which held them all together. She was now at the head of the family with Francis. She worked with the Grantley New York offices to organise and orchestrate Dorothea's funeral.

It was only when she stood against a French window and the light reflected, that Amber realised that Lucinda was pregnant!

She could not decide whether to be pleased or outraged. Her father was nearly 60 for heaven's sake. What right had he to be fathering children at that age? At 21 did she need a half-sibling?

Only then did she realise that if the child was a boy, it would take precedence over HER and become the Grantley heir. She had held that title for so long the idea came almost as a relief.

Dorothea's funeral took place with all due ceremony. The

great and the good all attended, paid their respects, ate the food and drank, with some additions, what had been ordered for Amber's party, then drove away.

"The end of an era," they murmured.

NOT QUITE – For Dorothea's will must be read.

The lawyers were sombre as they sat down with the family to disclose the contents of Dorothea's will.

It began with generous bequests to each of the staff, many of whom had worked for her for decades and were duly rewarded.

There followed gifts to her favourite charities.' Amber found herself impressed with the ritual of it all.

The sonorous sad voice of the lawyer intoning the words, the cast-down eyes of some of the listeners.

Bequests to her two sons-in-law came next, then a gift of fine jewellery and sums of money to each of her two daughters, Annette and Phillipa.

To Arabella Grantley of Courtneys, England she bequeathed her fine suite of emeralds and diamonds as a token of her regard.

She confirmed the right of her son, Francis Grantley, to the whole of the Grantley Corporation Industries, but expressed the hope that he would transfer Grantley Aeronautics to his sister, Annette and Grantley Automobiles to his sister, Phillipa, in recognition of their success in developing said companies.

To her son, Francis, she left her entire art collection with the fond hope that he would enjoy it during his lifetime, and then gift it to the nation.

To her beloved granddaughter, Amber Grantley, she left her estate of Fairhaven, and all the balance of her assets,

Dorothea had not known that she had another grandchild yet to be born, who would complicate matters.

To clarify, the lawyer confirmed that by Mr Randolph Grantley's will the whole of Grantley Industries had passed to Mr Francis Grantley.

Mrs Dorothea Grantley was merely expressing her wishes in the matter of the Automobile and Aeronautical Companies.

Mr Randolph Grantley had at the time of his death made generous bequests to each of his daughters. There had already been family trusts in place. However, he had made no specific bequest to his only grandchild.

Mrs Dorothea Grantley had now sought to correct this matter for the future Grantley heir.

Amber had given up listening and was mentally planning her next air challenge. All she was really concerned about was the future of Grantley Aeronautics.

It was understood that when Aunt Netty decided to retire, Amber would take over, but to manage it, not to own it. As the lawyer completed the reading everyone rose to their feet and were in need of refreshment. Mr Loveday asked Amber to remain behind.

"Miss Grantley, I wonder if you are aware of the value of your grandmother's bequest?"

"Not the slightest idea and I wasn't expecting her to leave me anything at all. That would be down to my father in the future."

"Under the terms of the will you will inherit 5 million dollars, plus the Fairhaven estate.
which we conservatively value at 8 million."

"But I don't want all that money!"

Amber burst out.

"I've always been given enough. My love, my education, my horses, my cars and now my plane. What do I want with all of that?"

"The capital is carefully invested. You are now responsible for the upkeep of Fairhaven, which will be costly. We are happy to act as your legal advisors. No doubt the Grantley Financial advisors will be available to you. Your alternative is to refuse the bequest when it would revert to your father Francis Grantley. The choice is yours. Please consider the matter most carefully."

Amber flew into the next room and burst out – "Oh everyone, I don't know where I am or what to do. It's all too much. Can we talk about it all tomorrow? I'm hungry, thirsty and tired and I bet you all feel the same."

They agreed, her father hugged her, and she left to visit Wing, who just nuzzled her.

CHAPTER 18
LONDON

Arabella returned to consciousness very slowly. It felt like passing through a dark tunnel with just a tiny speck of white at its end. As the light grew larger and brighter she at last escaped and slowly opened her eyes. Her eyesight was hazy at first.

A soft male voice encouraged her to wake up. Although the voice sounded vaguely familiar, it was hard to place. She saw first a nurse with a stark white uniform and cap.

"Good morning, Mrs Grantley. We're going to sit you up a little. You'll find it easier. Then I want to look at your operation wound and Nurse Chivers will dress it for you. First you need a drink, water then weak tea, please sip it slowly. I'll see you shortly."

"Thank you Dr Spiller" she murmured as he left her.

The nurse brought her drinks and also a bowl of water to sponge Arabella's face and hands, and a wide toothed comb to tidy her hair.

"Where am I, how did I get here, what has happened to me?," she asked the nurse.

"You are in a private room at St Thomas' Hospital. You were admitted seriously ill with what was peritonitis. Dr Spiller needed to operate at once as your appendix had ruptured and was badly infected."

"No more questions now. Just rest until the doctor returns and we check your wound."

Arabella sipped her tea and was decidedly puzzled. She had gone up to London to check the letters with suggestions for songs for her next wireless series. There was a shortlist drawn up by the musical advisor and several others with particularly poignant messages, which she might prefer to substitute. Arabella was seldom unwell. The last time she had been confined to bed was for Amber's difficult birth. How long had she been here? Would she be well enough to fly to America for Amber's 21st birthday celebrations? She had too many questions. It was all too confusing and she was suddenly very tired. Why was Robert here? She hadn't seen or heard from him since they had parted at Courtneys in 1918. Had she aged too much in the last 15 years? Had he?

She awoke as Nurse Chivers arrived with the dressings trolley. Her old dressing was removed and the area cleaned. Although a sheet was carefully placed to preserve her modesty she blushed as Robert carefully examined her.

"It's looking good and already healing nicely. I want you to rest for the remainder of today. You can have broth or soup and drink plenty of water, but no solids yet. It won't hurt to sit on the side of the bed."

Arabella looked away, as she knew that meant she could be assisted to a commode. It was all horrible and so different from the last time they had met, parting with kisses and suppressed desire.

"Doctor, I still don't know how I came to be in hospital. Can you please tell me?" The nurse departed and Robert quickly took her hand.

"Arabella, my dear dear girl. You suddenly complained of a fierce pain in your right side then promptly collapsed into unconsciousness. Did you not have any pains before this?"

"Oh I just thought it was indigestion and quite bearable. Shall I be fit to fly to America for my daughter's birthday?"

Robert looked at her gravely and told her that it would be impossible. The realisation struck Arabella that once more their mother/daughter bond would be broken.

"Perhaps she will be able to visit you?"

"Perhaps" replied Arabella glumly.

"Can I travel back to Courtneys with a nurse to help Bridie to look after me?"

"Not for a week at least. I'll bear that in mind. Meanwhile just do as we advise. Gentle exercise, rest, read and keep drinking and I'll add variety to your diet as soon as appropriate." Then he lifted her hand, turned it over and gently kissed her palm. He left her with his usual salute, 'Arabella', and a small bow. What a gentleman he was, but would he ever desire her now that he had seen her naked, helpless and scared? Why was life so unfair?

Then Arabella remembered those two strong women who had forged her. Her mother would have urged her to shake herself, count her blessings and work hard on her recovery. Her Aunt Alice would have told her to get Bridie to bring in her best nightdresses, dressing gowns and make-up. The sooner she looked better, the sooner she would feel better.

All jolly good advice. Then she realised if she left the

hospital, she would leave Robert too !

The three letters from America arrived by hand from Grantley's London office. Their contents were so unsettling that Arabella took a while and several readings to complete their contents.

Guy Winterton sat quietly whilst she read the first. Francis wrote to express his concerns for her health. Then he had to tell her that Amber had found her grandmother dead. Dorothea had passed quietly away, after a life well lived. They all missed her terribly at Fairhaven. Also, her death would inevitably result in many changes. Guy Winterton would keep her informed of any which would affect her. There was just one happy piece of news. Lucinda was expecting a child. Although she was 20 years younger than he, it was still so unexpected and they were both delighted. He concluded his letter with further good wishes for her recovery and the assurance that Grantley trust would pay her hospital bill.

"Oh good god" she burst out causing Guy Winterton to look up questioningly.

"Not Dorothea! she was just indestructible. Poor Francis and Amber will be heartbroken."

"Indeed so Mrs Grantley. I won't wait now. Please telephone me if there is anything you need. These are indeed painful times for the family".

Arabella wept bitter tears for Dorothea. She was a great lady. She had offered Arabella help and encouragement in her career and most of all taken over the responsibilities of bringing up Amber.

Arabella remembered the happy days of walking together in Fairhaven Gardens. The great collection of portraits she had formed would be Dorothea's memorial.

The attorneys letter informed her of Dorothea's bequest to her of her emerald and diamond suite.

"With my loving good wishes for your future happiness Arabella and gratitude for sharing Amber with me. She has been the light of my life.

I know that the emeralds are a little 'grand' for one's tastes, but they will enhance your beauty and later on Amber's.

Your affectionate

Dorothea"

The third letter was from her daughter.

For someone who seldom wept, Arabella's tears fell in floods. She drew a deep breath before she could face up to the letter from Amber. It was as she had expected, heart wrenching.

"Oh Mom, what am I to do without Granny, how can I go on without her? She has been with me ever since she came to Courtneys for my first birthday. She has loved me and guided me every step of my life and now I don't know what to do. Even flying doesn't help. I wish you were here, then we could comfort each other. The Aunts are kind, but Papa is taken up with Lucinda and now there is to be a new baby. I don't know yet how I feel about that and how you must feel. It seems somehow impossible after all the years when you and Papa didn't have more children.

Grandmother left <u>me</u> loads of money <u>and</u> Fairhaven, which is worth loads more. I don't know how Papa feels about that. Shall I give it back to him? Then he and Lucinda and the new baby would have what they expected to be his? I'm in such a puzzle what to do. I want to come over to see you, especially now you can't come to me as we promised each other. It is impossible with all the upheaval here. The attorneys are always meeting us, pressing for decisions about the corporation. Papa thinks there will be another war, so we must get everything right. I spend all my time in meetings instead of flying. I want to be in the air and reach for the sky and think that I must be nearer to grandmama up there. Is that stupid or fanciful or just part of grieving?

Please ring me as soon as you can, I long to hear your voice. I long to hear you sing again. Most of all I long for you to be well again. I couldn't bear to lose you as well. We may not see each other, but I know you are there and after grandmama, love me more than anyone else in my life.

Always

Amber"

This outpouring of emotions was so unlike her daughter that Arabella knew how distressed and uncertain Amber must be feeling. She had decisions to make which would colour her entire future and was ill-prepared to take them, as her whole life so far had been carefree and indulged by all the Grantley family.

Arabella booked a transatlantic call through to Amber at the first reasonable time.

When they were connected Amber burst into tears on

hearing her mother's voice. Arabella had schooled herself to be calm, to comfort and above all listen to the outpourings that she knew her effervescent daughter would produce. On that score she was perfectly correct!

"Oh Mama, what am I to do. I miss Granny so terribly".

"Darling Amber, you must do what we all do when someone precious dies. You mourn them, you remember them with love for the happiness they brought and you just carry on. I sang when my mother died. You must fly. But do it safely, as you always have. People will tell you the pain will get easier and somehow it does. Your life is of value, your grandmama lives on through you, because she brought you up. So live it for her as well and for me too."

"Gosh mom, that is such a help. You know what it's like too. I'll ring you tomorrow 'cos there'll be problems from the meeting with the attorneys.

Lots of love" – and the call ended.

If the death of Dorothea loomed large, the problems caused by her will were legion.

Meanwhile she enjoyed her daily consultation with Dr Spiller. He inspected her wound and agreed the levels of her food and exercises. By the next week she would be discharged to Courtneys under the care of Bridie and the local G.P. A live-in nurse was not considered necessary.

What was considered absolutely essential was the attendance of Dr Spiller each Sunday.

They met in dual roles. Doctor and patient. Co-conspirators

with light touches and meaningful glances. Arabella was a divorcee and Robert a widower. Their relationship could now blossom and be consummated once Arabella had fully recovered.

The attraction which had been born 15 years before had now gestated into the realisation that time was so fleeting and they needed each other. With their feelings assured, Arabella took time to consider how she viewed the news of Francis's impending fatherhood. He had been infertile for the whole of their marriage. Perhaps his period in captivity and the stimulus of a new much younger bride had proved a new fertility. She could not voice her fears, even to Robert. To do so would cast doubts on the legitimacy of Amber. So she did as she had always done and kept the secret of her daughter's real father. Only she knew that Richard Courtney's daredevil years lived on in their daughter.

She seemed to have been away from her wonderful home for far too long. In the few weeks of her illness, the gardens had burst into full bloom. The perfumes were heavenly as she meandered along the paths. She was still a little stooped after her surgery but knew that would pass and then …..

Bridie had worked her usual magic. The new head gardener had settled in and was working wonders. There were now 4 part-time maids. There was always laughter mixed with their hard work, and Bridie as ever handed out whiskey cake for guests and staff alike.

The wages bill was a little higher than anticipated, but her second series of 'Songs For You' would start in October. As the first had proved so successful, with high listening figures and her contract gave her much higher fees, she was due to cut five records and would be busy selecting the music with the record company. Things were looking up!

Francis wrote to her again, advising her to complete any outstanding repairs at Courntey's. She could expect support from Grantley's London, also to retain her staff at this time. He was now absolutely convinced there would be a war before the end of the decade.

Despite treaty restrictions, Hitler and his Air Minister Hermann Goring were managing to re-arm. Mussolini's air power and quality of planes was formidable. Both were dictators in effect, but had earned the support of their countries by improving conditions and promising future status in the world.

America was at last waking up to the situation. Boeing and Douglas were building prototype bombers already, while continuing to provide successful passenger and freight planes.

He wanted to warn Arabella so she could prepare for the future. England was so vulnerable.

Arabella had lived through one war. Surely there would not be another? They were still trying to find jobs for the unemployed and look forward to a brighter future. Perhaps Francis was being too pessimistic?

Robert's Sunday visits were the highlight of the week. They lunched simply in the garden pavilion, or on the terrace, or picnicked at the Dower House. This would be their special rendezvous when Arabella had regained her fitness. Each of them somehow knew that their commitment to each other was absolute, and their lovemaking would be at once tender then passionate.

By September, her recovery was complete. The Dower House was ready and so were they. In the golden glow of late afternoon, Arabella took Robert to bed at last. How could two people who had never made love together before now discover such wonderment and joy? This man who had seen so many bodies gloried in the lush beauty of Arabella. He stroked her golden limbs touching her where the sunlight caught her. She had worried too much about her long celibacy. It was discarded as carelessly as a rose petal.

She had known carnal love with Richard Courtney, ravished and bruised, but rising to him in her climax, impregnated by him.

She had known marital love with Francis, passion enforced so often after her too frequent absences. She had thought them well matched until the realisation that he could not father a child allowed silent frustration and resentment to undermine the marriage, despite her love for him.

Now in Robert and at a more mature age she had found everything. No romantic novel could have prepared her for the pure physical delights of her responses to him.

Robert's touches burst the dam of her pent-up desire. Her every cell strove to unite with his in an explosion of longing. Robert could not believe that the woman in his arms was at once so sweet and so passionate. He needed all his experience to satisfy her heat and passion. Each time they made love they were astonished at the depth and frequency of that desire. A part of his being as a man was the desperate need to possess and satisfy this woman.

121

At last they drew apart, sated and now languid with their lovemaking.

Whoever had said

Love's more comfortable the second time around

could not have experienced such desire as theirs.

Now what bliss to feel the sheer peace and comfort of lying together in total accord. They gazed at each other with tenderness.

They had experienced the primeval passions which had united man and woman since Adam and Eve and thanked their god for it.

Although the declaration was not really needed Robert asked Arabella to do him the honour of marrying him – and jolly soon too!

Arabella knew it would be too much for Amber following so swiftly on from Dorothea's death and Francis's marriage.

"Darling Robert, I know it will be hard to spend any more of our lives apart, but can you bear to wait until the new year?"

"Surely darling, but you'll be up in London for the week when you're recording and I can continue to visit you at Courtneys at the weekend. Meanwhile I'll give notice at the hospital and take leave at Christmas, but you must meet Amber very soon. She needs you."

Of course Robert was right and they sealed their bargain with a lingering kiss.

CHAPTER 19
PARIS

Arabella recognised the casually dressed glowing woman before Amber saw her. For a moment she thought she was mistaken. Could this tall assured young woman awaiting arrivals at Le Bourget be her daughter? The tilt to Amber's head, something in her eyes and the confidence born of wealth and status reminded her at once of Richard Courtney. So, the girl did take after her true father. Her figure was slender and very athletic. Only her fine skin and amber gold hair favoured her mother.

There was no timidity or restraint in their greeting, just a warm embrace and a kiss on each cheek.

"Oh Mom, I'm real glad to see you at last. Come on, I've got a cab waiting. We're in a suite at the Ritz and I've booked a special guide who knows the best places to stop for coffee and lunch. We've just got to explore. Then we'll have dinner at the hotel and talk and talk until two in the morning."

"Sounds wonderful darling" replied her mother. "I have performed at the opera house here and visited several art galleries, but let's do what you want to. It is easier for me to visit Paris. Was your flight too tiring?"

"Gosh no. I took a flight on one of the luxurious clippers. I may not care for seaplanes, but they've surely got the fuel capacity and comfort to make it over. Let's not worry about how long we've got, but just fill every moment."

 So began four unforgettable days with the daughter she had given over to Dorothea. Amber was a true Yankee, full of the energy and enthusiasms which categorized America and its people. Nothing was impossible and there was no problem that could not be solved by ingenuity and money. Now that Amber was 21 and wealthy in her own right, her magnetic personality and the confidence she emanated were intoxicating.

Their days were swept away in early starts, fuelled by coffee and croissants, which Amber ADORED. All the famous Paris landmarks were greeted with WOW or GOLLY or FABULOUS. Coffee and lunch breaks were not to be lingered over as they sped to their next famous destination. Both guide and driver knew to snatch a break before they were off again. Arabella never did get to visit the Louvre – 'Far too stuffy and that Mona Lisa is plain boring.'

Arabella did beg Amber to arrange a visit to Molyneux and Chanel. "Not likely, they'll only have snooty vandeuses who'll want to sell me silly frocks. I live in pants and sweaters or sleeveless blouses."

"I know darling, but the slacks will be perfectly cut with matching blazers or jackets. You'll be surprised how very stylish they are. Think how lovely it will be to return home with French Couture clothes. If we're quick they can fit you and send them to you either at the hotel or to Fairhaven.

Surely there is a young man you'd like to impress? Think how wonderful Marlene Dietrich and Katharine Hepburn look?"

"Sure, Sure" said Amber. "But I've got the fashion and dress department at a Hollywood Studio on tap and they're no slouches. I'll get the concierge to make an appointment. I bet they keep a list of wealthy Americans and the Grantley name should shake them up."

They weren't the only ones! Arabella had not associated her daughter's, smart but casual clothing with a Hollywood studio, more with clambering in and out of cockpits of aeroplanes. She looked at Amber enquiringly.

"O.K O.K I get it. Yes I've got a boyfriend called Chuck. He flies too, but not a patch on me. You saw the copy of the film I made? Well, I started to invest in the studio and own 50% of it. The profits have kept me going".

What a surprising girl Amber was, thought Arabella, much impressed by Ambers's acumen.

The swift appointment at Chanel confirmed Amber's financial status. The 'pants' and jackets she ordered were not only stylish, but of the finest materials and of enviable cut. She rejected the proffered braids, pearls and trimmings and ordered them plain and perfect.

Arabella asked if she could arrange an outing and Amber agreed and it was too late to protest when she found herself seated at the next mirror to her mother while their hair was cut and styled. Her rebellious glare might have intimidated a lesser man, but Monsieur knew what lay under his skilled hands. The resulting cut turned Amber into an icon of style. People turned to look at her. Surely she must be a famous model or film star?

"Gosh, gosh and gosh." If Arabella could turn her into a model perhaps her studio could turn her into a film star without an aeroplane. Think of all those gorgeous leading men!

With Dorothea's death and her father's re-marriage, Amber felt so alone. Boys and now men had always found her stunning. With her new maturity and wealth, she had decided to accept some of the offers. As long as the outings included fast cars, she was prepared to ward off some of their advances. Kisses and cuddles were O.K and a bit of fumbling to discover their anatomical differences. However, since she still refused to drink or get carried away, she changed her men as often as her planes. Thinking of Chuck made her feel warm and she surely missed him. Could he be THE ONE?

Crammed as they had been, the days had flown by. They had been served dinner in Amber's suite. Her questions had lain before them. The questions she must answer and even vote on at the next board meeting of Grantley's.

1. Did she agree with breaking up the Grantley Corporation into three distinct parts?
   No it would weaken the existing company and lay it open to predators as it had at Randolph's death.
2. What changes needed to be made in response to Francis's fears for a new war?

Amber had considered this carefully

> FIRST She would suggest – Lay up the vast stores of spares for their agricultural machinery business.
>
> THEN – Tool up again for the armaments in which they had specialised. Carry on Randolph's designs for tanks, but much lighter, mobile and well-armed, and armoured.
>
> BEGIN – Immediately to produce a two-seater trainer plane with specification approved by the War Department and establish a large training school for the would be pilots.
>
> THE AUTOMOBILE SECTION – Must be ready to provide sturdy all terrain military vehicles for the government.

If she could gain her fellow directors' approval then Francis, Penny and Annette could lead their separate businesses to huge advantage for the Grantley Industries Corporation.

It was only when they turned to Dorothea's bequest that Amber became uncertain.

"I can understand Grandma leaving me the money, but why the Fairhaven estate and shall I accept it?" she puzzled.

Arabella had thought a great deal about this.

"Do you think she had guessed that Lucinda was pregnant? If the child is a boy, you would be left with nothing, unless your father made full provision for you. Fairhaven has been your home for most of your life, so she determined it should be yours."

Why don't you ask Lucinda to carry on in charge of it, and ask for the expenses to be paid from the family trust? Speak to your father not in front of the others. Explain that you will be away frequently, so the change won't impinge on his family, nor the aunts."

Amber agreed on the plan, they slept, breakfasted quickly and Arabella waved her daughter off with a brave smile. Just as she was about to go. "Mama, it's time you married again. Don't be lonely now you are free. Grab life like I do! Love you." Off she went, a whirlwind of energy.

Arabella moved to a more modest hotel, then spent the day choosing her wedding outfit. Perhaps she should have confided her plans to Amber, but there had been so much to discuss.

When she returned to London two days later, she carried a most precious package.

CHAPTER 20
LOVE AND MARRIAGE

Arabella married Robert at the Kensington Registry Office one cool April morning.

The bride looked delightful in a Patou simple silk dress overlaid with lace. Her bouquet was of cream roses and she had a spray of lavender coloured leaves in her beautiful hair to add even more colour and sparkle to her vibrant violet eyes.

Bridie was her witness – who else!

She had helped Arabella to dress and exclaimed. "Sure you look swell enough to be marryin the Prince of Wales. Won't it be good to have a fellow back at Courtneys and him a doctor like my husband was? Here's to love." They laughed together like giddy schoolgirls, for that is what happiness does to you.

Robert and his witness Peter, a fellow medic, awaited them. Both were handsome enough to earn interested glances from other celebrants and Peter a very appreciative and speculative look from Bridie.

Robert surprised Arabella by placing not one but two rings on her finger. The first was a magnificent amethyst and diamond ring, then her gold wedding band. Vows exchanged and sealed with a kiss, it was time for lunch at the Ritz with all the opulence and style you could wish for.

Robert and Arabella decided to spend their honeymoon exploring Devon and Cornwall. Arabella even took the wheel of Robert's car and tootled along the winding lanes en route to their next hotel. Much time was spent enjoying the scenery and delighting in each other's company and their married status.

Their love was consummated frequently, and they returned to Courtneys to bring a new energy to that wonderful estate.

Arabella had thankfully told Amber of her impending marriage. A keen-eyed pressman had noticed the name Arabella Seymour Grantley on the list of marriages and what was a quiet wedding became national news.

The couple entertained and established new contacts and friends. Their first Christmas together saw Courtneys in full swing and looking just marvellous, aglow with lights, flowers, blazing fires and music. Arabella began to sing for her guests and put on a village concert too.

Robert worked at a nearby hospital, for medicine was too much a part of his life for him to be idle.

He discovered all the materials, easel, paints and high-quality brushes last used by Francis and began to paint when Arabella was in London.

The years flew by, but nothing could hide the news coming out of Germany. Francis had proved to be absolutely right. War was inevitable and the Allies, faced with a powerful enemy began the urgent task of re-arming.

All Winston Churchill's warnings, so often ignored, were coming true, yet the pacifists and appeasers could not be convinced.

Thankfully Sir Hugh Dowding, head of Fighter Command, convinced the government to concentrate on the production of Fighter aircraft and the installation of the Radio Warning System around Britain's coasts.

By 1938, 300 Spitfires were in service with the R.A.F along with the powerful Hurricanes.

Soon Britain would be at war with NAZI GERMANY with all RAF squadrons on war readiness.

On September 1st 1939 the AIR TRANSPORT AUXILIARY (ATA), was formed and AMBER WOULD SOON BE ON HER WAY TO ENGLAND.

CHAPTER 21
WAR – THE A.T.A 1941

Amber's love affair with flying had continued unhindered. She enjoyed the influence
and support of the Grantley name and business to sponsor her. Her prowess was well known, and she was offered planes from other companies to test – planes of all sizes and purposes.

She was most at home with Curtiss aircraft. It was a company which she had always admired. It was extremely successful, despite the untimely death of its charismatic owner. The American government bought its planes, and now so too did Britain and France in an attempt to catch up with the might of the German Airforce.

America was making huge sums of money with its sale of planes and armaments sent over to Europe, along with spares and engineers to train those servicing the planes.

Meanwhile, the pictures of the British Supermarine Spitfire made Amber's heart beat faster. Had there ever been a more beautiful aeroplane? How could she get to fly it?

Amber had vowed to fly in a war, and here it was. She must go to England to fight for the land of her birth. She must fight for her mother and help defeat an enemy whom her father described as evil.

Jaqueline Cochran was the pre-eminent woman pilot. If she supported and recruited in America for the Air Transport

Auxiliary, then that was good enough for Amber.

So here she was, leaving behind her cossetted life in America to become not Amber Grantley – aviatrix but a humble A.T.A ferry pilot Amber Seymour. Now she must make good her promise.

Bring it on!

The bus rattled its way through the lush green English countryside and eventually delivered the American pilots to a small airfield. It had several newly built brick buildings which were modern and warm. The mess greeted them with comfortable chairs, a warm palatable meal, hot sweet tea and abominable coffee. Their dormitories were functional and very clean. Each accommodated four pilots, who shared a bathroom. As they were all tuckered out with travelling a quick shower saw them soon in bed. Had they known it, this was to be the most comfortable reception they would receive!

Next day each was issued with a time chit for a medical taken between familiarisation lectures. Amber was photographed and given a National Identity Card. Another bus took the recruits to Luton for training. This was ground training. At first Amber was inclined to believe she would know it all, but so much was new to her. Navigation would be different. In America there were vast empty lands to overfly. In Britain, the cross-country flights were navigated from lower levels to allow identification of roads, railways, churches, towns, lakes, large landmarks. As the A.T.A. pilots had no radios to ask for assistance, all was visual. There was much to absorb and in map reading accuracy lay safety.

They were allocated billets with families. She and Honor settled happily at a farm with Farmer White, his wife Mavis and their two young children. Bicycles allowed them to explore the lanes and villages when off station.

Because she had flown some British planes in America, the instrument layouts were familiar to her, especially the large flat compass.

Amber worked steadily through the course; learning what was new and brushing up on what was familiar to her.

She spent time on aircraft recognition. If she was to fly in wartime with no armaments, then to identify an enemy plane and make a quick getaway would be crucial.

The A.T.A. might be regarded as a civilian organisation, but she doubted that a German pilot would take that into account if he spotted a lone British plane. Or that it was piloted by a woman.

The great Curtiss fighters had been bought by Britain and France in 1939 as they sought to re-arm to face the Nazi Forces. By then the Germans were already investigating jet-powered planes and arming their fighters with cannon as well as the more usual machine guns.   Perhaps Amber could fly a Curtiss soon?

Since their arrival in Britain the A.T.A. recruits had benefitted from good weather.   As the Tiger Moth and other first trainers were mainly open cockpit, this was a great bonus.

The recruits thrived.   They were kept informed by the 'Handling Notes' booklets for each type of plane giving them invaluable information.

Three weeks of ground school gave way to flying at last. Initial training on tiger Moths, Harvard and Miles planes led to advanced training at White Waltham, the A.T.A. H.Q. Even for Amber her first flight in a Hurricane caused her heart to leap with excitement.

The British were inventive, efficient, and well-disciplined. The greatest aid they had produced were small stiff cards secured at the top on two rings.   This fitted into a pocket on the knee of their flying overalls.   Each card gave the name of the plane and all the details which its pilot would need to fly it successfully.   The check list was impressive from hydraulics to unlock controls.   It chimed well with Amber's habit of constant checks.   The card became the A.T. A's bible.

The girls were quietly handed their wings with little

ceremony, to be sewn onto their smart navy A.T.A. uniform with its distinctive A.T.A. logo.

They were then dispersed to one of the ferry pools around the country. Only two were all women units, and Amber's was not one of them.

Amber felt great pride in her uniform and ordered a back up to be made at a London tailor, to be kept for dress occasions. Her striking hair was pinned up either under her flying helmet or jaunty side cap.

Used as she was to flying in America wearing very casual attire, she appreciated that the gravity of the war situation and the professionalism required demanded a very much smarter presentation.

The report sent to her Ferry Pool C.O. listed her skills as 'Outstanding,' and most unusually that in an emergency she could be used as a test pilot, a role she had played in America.

Her new billet was so lacking in comfort that Grantleys London office acquired a nearby cottage for her to share with Honor. Here they could be sure of warm water, fuel for the fires and a neighbour who was only too happy to provide domestic help. She would include some cooking services at a wage which would set her family up.

It surprised no one when Amber appeared at the base in a second-hand MG sports car. Why not! She had been driving since age 10 and flying since her 12th birthday. She would do her job better if she had slept in a comfortable bed, in a warm house and driven in her own car.   At first everything in England had seemed strange, even though they all spoke the same language.

Pounds with 240 pennies instead of dollars, nickels, and dimes. Small saloon cars instead of large automobiles, driving on the left-hand side of the road. Sooty, noisy trains, which chugged along and seemed to stop at every wayside station. There was rationing for almost everything, little heating and quite basic latrines and showers.

Amber soon developed the greatest regard for the British civilians she met. They in turn admired the spirited American girl who had come over to help win the war. They liked the fact that her English 'Mom' sang on the wireless.

They shared a determination to do whatever their country and their great Prime Minister, Winston Churchill, asked of them. The King and Queen were revered, and their subjects from their overseas countries arrived to fight for them. Despite the setbacks of Dunkirk and in the Middle East, everyone seemed confident of eventual victory. They would work all day, snatch a quick meal and then be off for the Home Guard, Fire Fighting or Air raid precaution duties until all hours.

They loved a pint of warm beer, a game of darts or dominoes, a sing-song or just a quiet pipe of tobacco at their local pub. Everyone seemed to smoke and go to the movies.

Their contempt for Hitler and the various names they gave him, and his troops amused Amber greatly. These were people worth fighting for. There were now three Eagle squadrons of American volunteers flying in Britain, yet still America resisted joining the Allies. There was a strong lobby for America to remain isolationist. OK to sell ships and p anes but not to put 'Our Boys' at risk.

This all came to a crashing end on December 8th, 1941, when the Japanese attacked Pearl Harbour with the loss of so much of the fleet, and so many lives.

At once many Americans returned home. Amber knew instinctively that she would remain here with the A.T.A. Their pilots would be needed more than ever for ferry cuties. Planes needed to be delivered to their squadrons as quickly as possible from the factories. Damaged planes needed to go to repair shops. Others needed upgrading, especially the constantly improving armaments.
All A.T.A. pilots reporting for duty were handed their chits. These stated what flights they would make that day. One would fly the taxi 'pick up' plane to return pilots to their

bases at the end of the day. Sometimes they would ferry a V.I.P. but rarely, as they carried no guns.

As part of her safety routine Amber liked to arrive early to study the meteorology boards. Nothing had equipped her for the rapid changes in British – especially Scottish – weather conditions. The wind direction could veer in a flash. The sun would be obscured by heavy rainclouds and lashing rain. A wispy mist could obscure the landmarks she sought. Worst of all was a fog, which enveloped the plane and disorientated the pilot. Once she had her chit she returned to the 'Met' boards for a final check. If conditions were too severe all flights were cancelled. This could result in days of inactivity in the mess or staying overnight at another airfield or base. Card games and conversation soon lost their appeal. Amber did not undertake any of the 'domestic' pursuits of knitting, crochet, embroidery, so she read. She chose British history so as to learn more of her mother's country. It fascinated her, and she discovered that others were less willing to interrupt someone deeply engrossed. Later there would be a meal, cards or darts, a drink for some, soft only for her. One or two of the more amorous chaps decided to make a move and were met with cool incredulity. They were still on duty. What they did on their six days a month off was their affair but would obviously not include her.

She managed to meet Arabella but infrequently. This made

their time together precious.   Amber would drive to London or meet her mother from the recording studio.   Sometimes she would be allowed to attend a 'Worker's Playtime' recording.   These were generally lively, even rowdy, recordings, usually in a factory producing munitions.   Yet when Arabella sang, there was always complete attention.   Her evocative music plucked at the heartstrings of her audience, reminding them of their distant loved ones, rather as her radio programmes did.   Although she was now over 60 Arabella always dressed with especial care, and took time to speak to as many of the audience as she could.

'Will you be able to visit Courtneys soon?' her mother asked.   'I've tried so hard to arrange it, but something always happens to stop my visit.   The best thing is to ring you and hope you are not in London recording.   I worry so much about you being caught in an air raid Mom.'
"I know darling, and I worry about your being in the air virtually every day.   Just phone or write whenever you can."

Then they would embrace 'Until the next time.'   Amber wrote every week to her father.   She was cautious with details for she knew the censor would intervene with his thick black pen.   The days when she received a reply really were special.   She knew as he always wrote by hand, that Francis was tired.   Like his father, Randolph, before him he had been caught in a war, when his every inclination was to spend more time with Lucinda and Jimmy, the son she had borne him in 1934.

At least the War Department had commandeered all aircraft companies, also the Grantley Automobile company, to make armoured vehicles.   Francis was still needed to conduct the Grantley main armaments production in conjunction with Government advisers.   Amber hoped that this would ease Francis's burden.

She ended every letter by sending love to Lucinda and Jimmy.   She was faintly concerned that his letters made little mention of his wife and child.

The weather conditions frequently interrupted duty days. When it at last cleared a few days before Christmas the backlog of planes waiting to be moved must be tackled, and all Christmas leave was cancelled.   Amber could not believe that she was to be thwarted yet again in visiting Courtneys, where she had been born.   Both she and Arabella were so upset.   Arabella's hopes and well laid plans for the Christmas together were in tatters.   Oh! This wretched war.

The new year brought more optimism and better news from the war zones.   The Germans would seize Crete and attack Russia, but old-style Swordfish planes managed to sink the great battleship Bismark.   The news bulletins and Pathe news- reels at the cinema were full of this massive success and a boost to Britain's morale.

Amber seemed to have been flying non-stop. Her few days off allowed her to catch up on laundry, sleeping, writing to her father. Visits to the cinema, as she now called the movies, and a Saturday night dance, became highlights. She looked forward to them as short periods of rest and recuperation in her hectic flying life.

Meanwhile her clearance levels had very quickly risen. Single engine fighters predominated, so her ambition to fly the wonderful Spitfire and its more heavily armed Hurricane, had been realised.

Her delivery chits became almost mundane, as so many fighters required ferrying from factory to squadrons, for Fighter Command needed them in large numbers. The Ministry for Aircraft Production had ensured their production line supply.

Amber had experienced some near accidents during so many years of flying. In America, the greatest hazard was running out of fuel by underestimating the huge distances. To compensate there was always an open space to make a safe forced landing.

Here in Britain the problems were faltering equipment and bad weather. The A.T.A. instructions were that if you are in trouble, you should put down immediately at the nearest airstrip. With no air/ground radio the pilot had to just risk it.

During one of her flights Amber was faced with a faulty – she hoped – fuel gauge, so she headed for the nearest air base.

As she emerged from a cloud formation, she saw a swarm of German planes attacking ground aircraft. Only a few Spitfires had managed to take off amongst the mayhem and destruction. As two of the Messerschmitt's peeled off they spotted Amber.

With practised skill one charged ahead and then turned on her, while the second took up station astern. Here she was. The unarmed 'meat in the sandwich.'

How easy to swot her down with their usual technique. This involved one plane flying directly at her on a collision course, lifting over her and her pursuer at the last possible second, when number two could riddle her plane with bullets.

Unfortunately for them Amber had flown this manoeuvre in a dare devil display for her film company. The result, on which her life depended rested on her holding her nerve, then quickly depressing her stick, and flying under the advancing plane.

The element of surprise was total. As she peeled away she sensed a huge collision between her enemies. Turning her Spit, she saw them embedded and spiralling to the ground.

Her vow to fly and fight like a Lafayette pilot had been realised.

Had they felt the same mixture of emotions which Amber felt? She alone had been responsible for the deaths of two young men, just as surely as if she had shot them! She experienced a feeling of despair then almost of exhilaration. They had gone to war aware of kill or be killed. They had just now killed men on the ground, not up in the clear air in fair combat. They were intent on killing her. Only her extraordinary skill and nerve had saved her.

Now would be a good time to land so she flew on to the next airfield on her route. While the ground crew checked her plane, she visited the mess for a comfort break, a cup of tea and a shortbread. Relieved of her flying overalls, hair tidied and lipstick applied she settled down with tea and a newspaper and a completely steady hand.

An orderly interrupted her –

'The C.O. would like to see you Ma'am if you'll follow me please.'

Amber was mystified. COs were usually far too busy with their station duties to worry about an unexpected landing by an A.T.A. pilot. Surely he could not have heard of her unusual encounter?

Equally unusual, he stood to greet her, and they exchanged salutes. She glanced at the name plate on his desk.

Squadron Leader Max Dickinson, it read.   The CO shook hands, seated her, and returned to his chair.   They sat in companiable silence sizing each other up.   She thought how very distinguished and handsome he looked.   Perhaps in his early 30's with wavy blond hair, deep blue eyes, strong chin and the faint look of fatigue which so many officers wore.

He in his turn saw a decidedly delicious woman whose determination and strength of character marked her out as special.

'Good afternoon, Officer Seymour.   I hope you're being looked after.   We've just been stood down from an aerodrome attack warning.   It is a good thing you came in before all my planes returned.   I'll ask the engineer to report to you as soon as he's located the fault.   Then you can decide if you have time to complete your delivery, or whether you need to stay here overnight as our guest.'

'Thank you' Amber replied gravely.   'That would be helpful. May I please ring my pool to let them know where I am, then again later when I know whether I can complete my delivery in time for the Anson to collect me?'

'By all means,' Max replied.
Amber could only think of him as Max.   She knew at once that they were destined for each other.   Please, please let him not be married.   She had been attracted to other men

of course, and had brief affairs, yet somehow, they both knew the indescribable feeling of connection, and where it must inevitably lead.

'I'll have to keep my line open, so the orderly will escort you to the main office. As soon as you have news of your plane, will you come here please?'
The formal words did little to hide his true meaning.

'Of course,' she nodded and left. Gosh she'd forgotten to salute him!

The Spitfires began to return to base. There was the usual hubbub after the debriefing. The marauding raiders had been intercepted and two of them shot down. But it was the exploits of the loan unidentified Spit which had accounted for two of the enemy without a shot being fired which astonished them. The news had come in and everyone was anxious to meet him, slap him on the shoulder and buy him a drink. Amber sat quietly behind her newspaper with a fresh pot of tea and a sandwich, listened and smiled to herself.

The fitter reported that her fuel gauge required a spare and would be available next morning.

Amber reported to her pool C.O., collected her bag, and prepared for an overnighter at the nearest convenient

accommodation.   When she reported back to Squadron
Leader Dickinson, he had received the news.
'I've had them book you in at the King's Head in Hornchurch.
I'd like to drive you there myself and give you dinner.   A
driver from the base will collect you at 8.30am tomorrow.
Will that be OK?'

'Absolutely, thank you, as long as you don't mind waiting
while I freshen up?'

As they set off in his lively but unflashy car Amber realised
that her life was about to enter a new chapter.   She
determined to relish the changes which Max would surely
introduce.

They lingered over a surprisingly good dinner.   He was
known and his rank obviously counted for some special
treatment.

Amber had rushed her bath to concentrate on her makeup.
Sadly, her overnight bag contained only fresh underwear and
clean shirt, so no dazzling dress, just her smart well-brushed
uniform.   It was enough.   Their conversation flowed as they
learned of each other's background.   Max loved flying as
much as Amber but had come to it much later.   His rapid
promotion owed much to his flair, tempered by good
judgement and management skills.

Amber was proud to tell him that she was also cleared to fly light bombers and heavy bombers. She longed to pilot a Lancaster bomber soon but had no ambition to move to level six and seaplanes.

As the meal neared its end their conversation faltered as soft looks and touching hands took over. The need in both of them was palpable, yet it was impossible for him to stay with her. They walked to his car and clung to each other exchanging the sort of kisses she had only seen on screen. God, he was gorgeous! He moved with the easy grace of an athlete, and she knew he would be a terrific dancer. All they needed to do was to find a weekend when they could drive off to a land of discovery and delight.

As he returned her to the hotel entrance, he said quietly, 'I don't know how you did it, Amber, but it was a truly marvellous manoeuvre. Perhaps you'll tell me how when we next meet.'

'Fine, if you'll tell me whether my fuel gauge really needed an overnight repair.'

'You're on' he laughed as he opened the door, gave her a cheery wave, and left her.

CHAPTER 22
FRANCIS GRANTLEY

Francis fingered Amber's latest letter with keen anticipation. Its arrival would enliven his day, and his secretaries knew that he was not to be disturbed – except by the President of the United States or the Secretary of State Department.

Francis was an exhausted and saddened man.   He had adored Arabella, and his fearless daughter Amber.   He had been at the top of his business and professional life heading a great and powerful Corporation.   Now, as his father Randolph had before him, he felt trapped in the coils of the demands of a war.   This time America itself was directly involved, and his dream of retiring to a peaceful life with his second wife Lucinda and their son had vanished.   As a true patriot he must continue in his role until the ghastly war ended, then he could begin to realise his long-held ambition to paint again, and to enjoy family life.   As Arabella had chosen to live in England, he had sadly divorced her, and married Lucinda.   Their longed-for son had ensured a male heir for him.   Why then did he feel uneasy?

There had been a subtle change in Lucinda since his mother in her will had left their home Fairhaven to Amber.   His wife fulfilled all the duties of chatelaine, yet there was a lack of warmth and companionship he had hoped for.   He had acknowledged Jimmy as his heir over Amber, but it was not enough to satisfy her. She accepted the respect due to any Grantley family member, the jewels, and gifts he lavished her with, her position as a great hostess – and yet she still looked at him with indifference. Because Francis was so much at work, he had been unable to establish a close father-son relationship with Jimmy. He thought of his own sometimes gruff father who had lavished both praise and criticism on Francis in equal measure, but always with the bear hug which said

'I love you son.' Perhaps Francis was just too old.

Suppressing a sigh, he slit open the envelope and withdrew the letter from his ebullient daughter.

'Dear Pops

How're you doing? I miss you lots, more than ever in fact now I've got so much news to share with you. Most of it won't escape the censor so you'll need to read between the black pencil words. You can do it! You know that I've flown S & H and several American planes used over here. Some easy, some not.

I'm cleared for the next two levels (you'll have to look them up). It is the greatest thrill, yet very challenging. On days of horrid weather, I long to be in the blue skies of California, then land and meet a film star for dinner. Wouldn't that be something? Best of all would be to meet you, my beloved 'Pops.' To yarn like we used to, then turn to all the business decisions and solve them in a flash.

I want you to send me a photo, so I can talk to you while I'm off duty. You know when I'm airborne I keep my mind strictly on the job. I've had a few hairy moments lately, and long to share them with you. I <u>can</u> tell you that I have recently met an RAF officer. We hit it off at once. His name is MAX and he is just GORGEOUS. Watch this space as they say!!!

Will this wretched war never end so that I can bring him over to introduce him to you all? Then he'll see my background to account for my confidence and free spirit (he says).

They are down to you and Mom. To your patience when I was a pain, to your encouragement of my sense of wanting to race autos and fly planes. I can't ever thank you both enough. You've been – and are – terrific. I saw Mom in London. We had supper together. She seems happy with Robert, but like you they are both too busy. Doctors are in short supply, and Mom is either recording or giving concerts for civvies and service men (and women).

I've still not made it to Courtneys, which seem impossible after so long in England.

I miss sheer stockings, nice cosmetics, warm underwear, magazines, and sunshine. I've asked your London office for some goodies and canned goods, so we'll see if they can oblige.

Do look after yourself darling Pops,
          Your loving daughter
                Amber
          XXXXX – by the dozen!'

Francis laughed out loud at his daughter's ebullient letter. How he longed for her to burst into his office, a whirlwind of energy and ideas.   Sadly, that happy moment must await the end of the war.   He also realised that for the first time ever she had not sent love to Lucinda and Jimmy.   He must be careful to mention them warmly when he next wrote. Amber's lively loving letter did re-enforce something he had been intending to do but had put off.   Buzzing his secretary, he asked her to make an immediate – that is today please – appointment with his lawyer, and in his lunch hour if possible.

It was, and Francis handed over his requirements.   As they shook hands Francis said,
'Now Willett, I've decided on just clarifying a few items in my will.   I wish these changes to be dealt with at once.   Can you deal with it and send it over to me and sign and have witnessed?'
'Sure can Francis, but please sit while I read through them and check that they are all practicable.'

He raised his eyebrows as he read some of Francis's startling bequests.

1. To my former wife, Arabella Seymour Grantley Spiller, the sum of one million dollars to replace the allowance which is currently made to her annually.
2. To my daughter, Amber Aurora Dorothea Evelyn Grantley, the sum of five million dollars. I also confirm her right to the ownership of our family estate at Fairhaven, as willed by my mother Dorothea Grantley.
3. To my wife, Lucinda Grantley, I give the sum of twenty million dollars for her comfort and maintenance.
4. To my son, James Randolph Grantley, the interest in Grantley Industries Corporation when he attains the age of 21 years.
5. The entire remainder of my estate to my daughter, the said Amber Grantley.

Willett looked at Francis with some puzzlement.

'Are you entirely sure Francis?'

'Entirely, I just need to know there are no legal loopholes to challenge it by any of the recipients. Anyway. draw it up, let's get it signed. Then if you suspect any problems we can amend it.'

'Will do,' replied Willett in his 'can do' Yankee way.

'Get your girl to make an appointment for next week. We'll meet at the Waldorf, and I'll confirm. It does occur to me that your daughter is flying in England in wartime. God forbid, but should she be killed, you may want to think of an alternative to her bequest.'

'I'll send you a note on the matter before we meet' said Francis. Rising to shake hands and make his departure.

He felt a great deal lighter and happier now, more so when he signed the document, and it was witnessed by two staff members.

Jimmy's education and allowances had been covered in the main document.   Now his beloved Amber would be secure and wealthy.

He decided to give Tiffany's a call and buy Lucinda a gift on his way home.   That should bring a light to her eyes and a little warmth to his bed.

CHAPTER 23
AMBER – HIGH FLYER

When she had delivered her Spitfire, flown a Hawker Typhoon to repair unit and returned to her pool, Amber expected a leisurely evening, but there was a message for her to report immediately to the CO.

"Take a seat please. I have some important information for you. I know that you have flown Beaufighters, Wellingtons and Hampdens. Now – I have an unusual request – that you ferry a Lancaster from advanced repair to Scampton. A flight engineer will accompany you. Then you will have a chit to transfer to White Waltham H.Q.

I see that you are due a 48 hour leave, so you may want to take it in London. Following that, you are to return to White Waltham for further instructions, which I am not privy to. You may take a suitcase instead of your overnight bag.

Use the rest of this evening to familiarise yourself with the handling notes. It is a great responsibility, but I am confident you can handle it.

Report in an hour early when a pool driver will deliver you to the airfield. These are demanding times for aircrew."

'Yes sir' replied Amber respectfully.

He dismissed a puzzled Amber.   Only a very few English A.T.A. women had flown a Lancaster.   How strange that her dearest wish was to be granted so soon after expressing it to Max.   Surely his influence did not extend to the A.T.A. command?   As conjecture was useless, she retired to her room to study every aspect of Lancaster handling.

The plane was massive, far bigger than she had imagined seeing diagrams and photographs, and in flight.   It carried along with its huge airframe and four Merlin engines, a kind of majesty, which outshone any other plane.   Amber loved it at once.

She shook hands with her flight engineer, Barry Richards, and they completed their visual check before boarding.   Did she imagine the same speculative look which she had noticed in her CO?

They climbed the ladder to board the plane.   Amber was startled to see the pilot's seat already occupied.

"Good morning, Officer Seymour.   I'm pilot instructor Peter Richardson.   You must complete four flights under instruction before you can become pilot Captain of a Lancaster.   Let's start with all the checks, shall we?"
The sequence was embedded in Amber's mind, but she had to patiently observe the Captain running through them. With four engines this took time.   She strapped herself into

a seat while he took off smoothly and headed north.

"I'm taking you cross country and then we'll turn for the delivery. I'll expect you to observe carefully and be ready to ask or answer questions."

After 30 minutes he handed the controls to Amber, to her absolute amazement. She stayed calm and steady, correcting pitch, maintain height and speed and feeling the plane in her usual ritual. Captain Richardson made a few suggestions enroute. Her time flew by quite literally. Soon enough they were approaching their destination.

'Take her down now please,' and so she did just that, with complete competence.

'Well done, said her instructor as she taxied to the holding area. 'I hope to see you again soon.'

She had expected to feel elated, yet she handed in her chit, grabbed a coffee and biscuit, then took off for White Waltham, the A.T.A. HQ, piloting a Puss Moth. So, from a Goliath to a butterfly in one day. No room for egos in the A.T.A. girls!

When Amber handed in her chit she was given two messages. The first was in response to hers to Max on the previous evening. It read Can do. Meet at the Savoy

Saturday lunch. Be prepared!

Did this enigmatic note mean be prepared for lunch in the Savoy Grill, or for afters? Probably both.

The second was a letter requesting that Officer Seymour attend a meeting that evening with the CO and others at 6.30p.m.

Amber was somewhat puzzled by the 'and others' but would soon know what was on hand. Meanwhile she could just relax and dream of the morrow and the gorgeous Max.

She had extolled his good looks and appeal in letters to both of her parents. When Arabella read her letter, her own mother's words rang in her ears,
'Handsome is as handsome does.'
Then Arabella wondered how soon she would meet this paragon of all the manly virtues and hoped for Amber's sake not to be disappointed.

Her daughter was meanwhile donning her best uniform, with crisp fresh shirt. With hair brushed and freshly pinned in place she was prepared for her meeting with the CO and the ominous 'others.'
She entered the office and stood smartly to attention as she was introduced to the three men seated there. Only the senior RAF officer's name was divulged. The two civilians

were identified as representatives of the GRAHAME Aircraft company.

They were of pleasant but unremarkable appearance.

Once Amber was seated, the CO began – "I must emphasise that everything we discuss is top secret. Is that understood, Officer Seymour?"

"Indeed Sir, of course," Amber replied.

The RAF officer then asked.

"First can you confirm that you were piloting a Spitfire Mark IX when you caused a collision between two Messerschmitt B.F. 109's?"

"I did Sir" she replied steadily.

'Yet you have made no attempt to report the incident?'

'No Sir, I am a ferry pilot, not a combatant.'

'Indeed so, but astonishing, nevertheless. We also note that you have always received 'Exceptional' as your rating, also your extensive flying hours and experience as a Grantley test pilot in America.'

One of the GRAHAME Company representatives began to explain the reason for the meeting. The jet engine invented by Frank Whittle was now essential to keep Britain abreast with Germany in fighter warfare. Germany had forged ahead and now had a full squadron of jet aircraft.

'Only four jet aircraft have joined our operations. We have a plane that can reach over 475 mph and climb to a 40,000-

foot ceiling. However, it is proving unreliable and the margin for pilot error is small. We have recently lost two planes, with their pilots. We need someone experienced to test the plane and identify the gremlin. Could you assist us? It may not sound an appealing mission, but could you help us? You would be listed as a volunteer. You can study all the detailed reports, and my colleague will help with any questions you have. These details are not to leave this room.'

Amber had been both puzzled and intrigued when she entered the room, but also somewhat apprehensive. What might appear to be an unreasonable request she regarded as a challenge to her skill and experience. Following a short pause she said,
'If I start now, I can do three hours, then continue on Monday when I return from leave. Does that suit you Sir?'

The other boffin nodded agreement, and he and Amber set to work as the others left them to it, with the promise of regular food and coffee. She and the quietly spoken Richard, as he introduced himself, worked steadily through the reports which Amber frequently questioned.

At 9.30p.m. she stood, stretched, bade him 'Goodnight', and left. She had already made up her mind to accept the challenge. She might have fulfilled her early pledge to test fly Grantley planes, but this was war, and a whole new ball game.

CHAPTER 24
THIS MUST BE LOVE

Amber was already in a mood of delight. The White Waltham pool driver had dropped her at a Mayfair hair salon for a late-booked appointment courtesy of Grantley's London office. It was spot on time. She left 1½ hours later in a taxi for the Savoy. Her golden red hair glistened in an elegant style ready to convert into bouncy curls should she wish. Her uniform slacks had been replaced by a smart skirt enhanced by dark fine stockings and court shoes. She looked both glamorous and efficient.

When the receptionist saw the wings on her uniform, he immediately upgraded her room to a suite for this highly desirable guest.
'Would Madam care to take coffee until Squadron Leader Dickinson arrives? Your luggage will be taken to your room and unpacked for you.'
Indeed, Amber would. She admired the white grand piano in the centre of the grand room where 'Hutch' and many famous bands performed. Max's lovely low drawl interrupted her immersion in the daily newspaper.

'Hello darling. How smart you look, really a knockout. Let me have a coffee, and then we'll have a spot of lunch in the Grill.'

How debonair Max looked.   He was the epitome of everything a dashing RAF officer should be.   Some fellow guests even speculated that he might even be a film star!

The Government had realised the power of films to project the value of the country's armed forces.   A steady stream of films featuring well known actors drew large crowds and boosted the public morale in the face of Germany's onslaughts.

Amber and Max were seated prominently in the famous dining room.   Their luncheon was served by elderly waiters drawn out of retirement.   They knew their jobs and performed them apparently effortlessly.   The couple both chose smoked salmon with asparagus followed by lamb and spring vegetables.   No dessert, just some real coffee.   All utterly delicious.

'Before we change out of uniform I want to take you somewhere,' Max told her.
'It's an old established place which my family has patronised for yonks.'   He was soon ushering her into a jeweller in the ornate Burlington Arcade.

They were courteously escorted to the manager's inner office.   Here laid out for them were several trays of rings. Amber was startled.   Is this what Max's enigmatic 'Be prepared' in his message was all about?   Amber rather hoped he had proposed to her first!   Had she wished to refuse him it would have been awkward.   What a thought to entertain when she had fallen so madly in love.

With a perplexed smile from her, and 'Wizzo' enthusiasm from Max, they inspected the rings as the finer points of each were explained.

'Which do you prefer Darling?   Just choose your favourite.' Amber tried each on as the jeweller handed them to her. They were all quite elaborate with large gems in ornate settings.

Amber could not tell Max that she held in a New York bank all the jewels from Dorothea, which she never wore.   Now she asked to see a simpler collection and immediately loved a smaller but exquisitely cut solitaire diamond on a platinum setting and band.

'Perfect choice Madam,' said Mr Latimer as Max kissed her hand before she passed the ring back to him.

The carefully wrapped box was handed to Max, and they left with many felicitations.   She did notice that no payment was made, and presumed there was some private arrangement in place.

Back at the Savoy, they separated to 'freshen up.'   Amber was impressed.   Not only had her suitcase been unpacked, but her dresses had been pressed to remove any creases.

166

Her underwear was laid out in the drawers and her nightdress laid out on the large bed. Not even the Ritz in Paris had done it better.

Unsure what the next move was to be she retained her stockings, silk and lace bra and French knickers covered by a silk dressing gown.

There was a brisk knock on the door which connected to the next room. Max breezed in and said 'Not dressed yet darling. I thought you might enjoy a stroll along the embankment, then we'll have tea before bath and change for dinner and dancing.'

Amber was nonplussed. She had expected to be in bed naked admiring her newly presented ring alongside her gallant lover. Oh well, at least she'd be able to assess his dancing skills. 'Be prepared' had obviously not been reached yet!
Her smart suit and pill-box hat won Max's approval, and they strolled along in happy accord discovering so much in common with their aviation backgrounds. As Amber Seymour she had decided to keep the secret of her real identity, cautious that the Grantley name would disclose her status and undoubted wealth.

They dawdled, held hands, watched the Thames and fellow walkers, and stopped to kiss as lovers do. Tea was taken back at the Savoy as a pianist played the latest hits. It was such a relaxing and delightful break from the responsibilities and anxieties of war.

Max and Amber made a glamorous couple as they came down to dinner, where they joined a crowd of fellow diners intent on forgetting the war with carefree laughter and music and good food.

Amber took a small sip of the champagne Max had ordered as he proposed a toast,
'To us Darling, and a splendid future.'
'To us Max and thank you so much for arranging this wonderful weekend.'
'No more than you deserve dearest.'

They rose to dance between courses, and Max was indeed a swell dancer. His sense of rhythm ran through him, and he communicated it to her as he led her skillfully around the small dance floor. He held her close in the slow dances and she felt the heat of his body through the thin silk/satin bias-cut dress she wore. She saw other women casting envious glances at them. How they would have welcomed being in the arms of such an expert and handsome partner.
At last Max finished off the last of the champagne, took a small whisky nightcap, and then escorted her to her room.

'Won't be long darling,' he said. He was true to his word,

and she barely had time to change into her very glamorous nightdress and brush her teeth and hair before he appeared.

Wasting no time, he lifted her in his arms and carried her to the bed.   He produced the box containing the ring and slipped it onto her finger.
'Marry me please my love.   You know I adore you.   Things are hotting up and we'll be busier than ever.   Please let's not wait.   Tomorrow wouldn't be too soon for me, but I know you'll need to organise it all.'
With a lingering kiss and a murmured
'Oh, Max I'd love to,'
Amber gave herself up to his embraces.   He was totally confident of his masculinity and its appeal to so many previous conquests.   He pressed all the right buttons, whispered all the usual endearments, and at last made feverish love to her.

Sadly, his words
'Won't be long' proved prophetic.
Before Amber had even begun to adapt to his rhythm he sighed contentedly, rolled from her and with a 'Wonderful darling Amber'
fell soundly asleep.

'Golly gosh – and I've just agreed to marry him!'
She did indeed sit propped against her pillows admiring her engagement ring, but under circumstances she could never

have envisaged. Perhaps Max had drunk too much or was just too excited. Only time would tell.

When she awoke and stretched out sleepily Max was not there ready to make love to her as she lay in tumbled languor.

There was a knock at the door and a waiter wheeled in a trolley set with breakfast for two. Max appeared fully dressed, kissed her warmly and helped her into her dressing gown. He seemed quite unaware or unconcerned about their mis-matched performance the previous night. The coffee perked him up even more.
'Buck up darling, I'm taking you to the country. Let's aim to leave by 10.30am.'

With that he was off, whistling cheerfully to himself. Amber 'bucked up' and completed her toilette. She chose navy blue slacks, a white blouse a scarlet jacket with white braid. A jaunty red beret completed her outfit.

'Very patriotic' Max commented admiringly.

Amber noticed that at the desk he thanked the receptionist but paid no money. As he left her to reclaim his car and supervise their luggage she asked for her bill.
'Oh no madam. The Squadron Leader has asked for it to go on his uncle's account.'

Max was back before she might ask the name of this generous chap.

The Complete Angler at Marlow was the personification of an English riverside hostelry. Punts and rowing boats were meandering along the Thames, and the sun shone warmly. How Amber wished that more of her flying days enjoyed such perfect weather. Suddenly she felt an overwhelming homesickness for American skies and her American family. Had she even mentioned to Max her intention to return there after the war and take control of Grantley Air Industries. Why did she hold back?

Of course she was forbidden to tell him of her test flights. She hugged the secrets to herself. He would need to be 'prepared' for some surprises too.

They strolled along the towpath while Max explained the finer points of rowing to her. She forebore to mention that both her uncles had rowed for the USA at Olympic level and then sailed in the America's Cup Races.

'Time for a spot of lunch Darling.'
'Great' she replied enthusiastically. All they seemed to have achieved was walking, dancing, dining, and motoring; and Max seemed unconcerned at the omission of real intimacy.

A flustered receptionist awaited them.

'We've been searching for you Squadron Leader. You've an urgent message to return to base immediately. Your luggage is ready, and I've brought your car round.'

'That's jolly decent and quick-thinking of you,' said Max exercising all his charm. He slipped the man a pound note and they drove off. He dropped her back to

White Waltham with a kiss, and a 'Cheerio old bean, I'll ring you when the flap is over.'

With her romantic weekend in tatters Amber changed into her uniform and returned to the CO's office, where she spent the remainder of the day studying the plane's papers and preparing her questions for the following day.

The meeting with the Grahame boffin was brisk and fruitful.

When she'd examined all the technical and engineering details, her questions were clearly answered. In addition, she wanted to see the latest reports from the surviving test pilot, which did not seem to be there.

Also, she wanted to fly a Mosquito every day to become used to the level of speed she expected to experience.

Finally, she asked for a visit to the Grahame Factory before she inspected the completed jet.

Factory and Farnborough lay ahead.

CHAPTER 25
ARABELLA

Arabella opened the letter happily as she recognised her daughter's bold writing.

The news it contained was joyful. Max had proposed, presented her with a splendid engagement ring, AND they wanted to be married at Courtneys asap – or sooner!

Could Arabella make all the arrangements with the vicar – details enclosed for the banns? Amber would forward the date as soon as the RAF could give them leave, and the numbers to be invited would follow.

It would be a typical wartime wedding, but a little more sophisticated if Arabella and Bridie could manage it all – a sort of summer idyll allowing a break from the anxieties and responsibilities of service life.

I know it's asking a great deal of you all, she wrote, I've waited so long to marry that I long for it to be SPECIAL to Max and me, and for all our guests.

You'll make a smashing Mother of the Bride, Mom, and you must invite some of your friends and neighbours too. It will be great to meet them.

I've wired Pop and at last managed to speak with him.   He's delighted for us, but it will be impossible for him to make the journey over.
How sad is that?

Would Robert give me away please, I'd like that?

Amber sounded a little frenzied, so unlike her usual self.   It must be the excitement of it all.   Yet why on earth did Arabella feel so uneasy?

Max was obviously personable, an officer and a gentleman. If only she and Robert could have met him.   She trusted her husband's judgement.   Was it their task to approve Amber's choice?   Of course not, yet both Arabella's mother and Bridie had been takin in by plausible rascals.   She couldn't let it happen to Amber.

She must tell Bridie at once.   They would sit down together over a pot of tea and start on the lists.   If the wedding could be anything like her's to Francis, it would be just perfect.

The weather was bound to be brilliant, and the gardens were looking well and productive.
Finch's rose garden remained unspoiled, and Arabella cared for it and guarded it fiercely.   Perhaps the now slightly faded blue and white pavilion would become a favourite place for Max and Amber as it had been for her parents.

CHAPTER 26
BRIDIE

'Sure, I can't believe me own ears. A wedding and Miss Amber to be the bride. Sure, won't that be grand. We'll have the best time, so we will. Let's be getting at the lists Miss Arabella, for we can crack it in a flash with the right lists. I'm going to have to get me hair dyed and sort out me finery too. I'll want to spread me Irish charm among all the lovely chaps who'll be there.'

Arabella laughed out loud, set aside her concerns and indeed they got at the lists, and it was fun as ever with dear Bridie.

Bridie thanked her lucky stars that after her failed second marriage, she had returned to Courtneys and Arabella, in her old post as House Manager.

Sure, it was no picnic running the house in wartime. Coupons for everything, shortages of everything, make do and mend as things wore out and couldn't be replaced. Still, she managed it all and laughed and sang her Irish songs to help them all keep cheerful. Mr. Robert was away to the hospital and Miss Arabella off to the singing. Sometimes she needed Bridie to go with her to London and they saw the bomb damage. Yet they met the invincible workers who just kept going.

Miss Arabella sang her heart out, and Bridie made sure she always looked grand. There were few dainty meals in their hotel. More often than not it was a canteen lunch and a fish and chip supper.

Now when they were away overnight the lists kept them busy and happy.

The vicar had been alerted, the banns read for the first time of asking and the choir and order of service settled. Only the date was still lacking.

Two of the maids had left to work in munitions with very generous overtime rates while the remaining two worked their socks off.

John Webster, the orderly who had stayed at Courtneys after WW1, took over all the clerical work of ordering Bridie's requirements. His letter clearly stated that bride and groom were both pilots.

Sure, they'll be madly in love and this war isn't over yet, with both of them facing the dreaded Hun, for them Luftwaffe men are cruelly dangerous. We're bound to give them a great wedding to remember. Most of her suppliers agreed and the lists showed many ticks.

Bridie had no compunction in enlisting the help of Grantley's

London Office.

Sure, and wasn't Miss Amber one of the family and hadn't America still the greatest luxuries? She remembered the famous hampers which Mr Francis used to order from Fortnum and Mason…Now even they hadn't much to supply, but Bridie fully expected that Grantleys London could work miracles with Grantleys New York.

Their list started with all the champagne and wines!
Bridie and Arabella had planned a famous feast. The estate farms would give up their bounty and Courtneys Garden too. What could better home-grown strawberries and bowls of freshly whisked cream?

Bridie thought wistfully of her handsome airman son. Eddy had been posted to Canada. She longed for his return. When would he find a lovely girl to marry? 'Safety in numbers' he'd laughed, but Bridie longed to be a grandma.

CHAPTER 27
AMBER'S GREAT ADVENTURE

Amber was living her life in a state of suppressed excitement. She had cast aside any doubts about Max's sexual shortcomings, making loads of mental excuses for him. No one could be that gorgeous and be unable to put it into action.

Their wedding plans in the capable hands of her mother, and Bridie, were all on schedule and sounded spiffing.

Now all such consideration must be set aside. SHE, yes, she, Amber Seymour had been selected to test this most amazing craft. All her energy, experience and knowledge must be channelled into the latest and biggest challenge.

Amber had quietly transferred to Cheltenham to visit the GJ500 factory there.
She watched the production line in every detail and was permitted to question the workers. For two full days she looked, questioned, and learned as she had done at the Grantley Burbank works in what seemed a lifetime ago.

When she saw the completed aircraft, she found it very compact. The pilot was seated forward and had excellent visibility.

Snub nosed, and without propellers, it surely was a new concept in aircraft development since Frank Whittle had first produced his jet engine. He had received an award of £10,000 from a grateful government to reward his inventiveness.

Reporting for duty at Farnborough, she first took up a Mosquito; a type which she had flown several times before. Manoeuvrable and very fast, she used it to sharpen her reactions.

After two days Amber was ready to face the GJ500. She sat in the cockpit and first checked that the seat straps were tight enough to keep her secure. Then she inspected all the instruments minutely and went through her check list.

This was not a plane to be taxied. Once the engines were activated, she sped along the long runway and eased back the stick more forcefully than she had expected, for the controls were heavier.

She was scheduled to spend time on a settled series of manoeuvres and was in radio contact with the control tower. First straight passes followed by swift changes of direction as would be required in aerial combat. This was to be followed by climbing to 30,000 feet, a steady descent, then a steep climb and descent at top speed before levelling out and landing.

The sheer thrill of building up to nearly 500mph and 38,000 feet was breathtaking. Amber realised that she was probably the first woman pilot to achieve them. After two further flights she was ready to submit her report.

She noted that speed and climbing abilities which gave any aircraft huge advantages, were exceptional. The pilots would need to be experienced and to be allowed proper time to train on the plane before combat duties. There was so little time at such high speeds to correct pilot error. She identified several small technical problems. The main gremlin was a problem with the fuel supply which unless resolved would cause the plane to fall from the sky.

Nearing the top of her second climb Amber had felt the engine becoming under powered. The problem would only worsen when the weight of armaments was added. She immediately pulled out of the climb.

At near vertical, the fuel was not pumping through correctly. It needed investigating to find the fault and also the fuel itself would need to be re-assessed.

The questions from the engineers and boffins continued for what seemed like hours. She answered briskly, offering facts not speculation.

At last, she was formally thanked, given a meal, and allowed to return to her pool at Aston Down.

Amber had felt no fear.   Two previous pilots had died in
their planes for sure, but she had been too busy
concentrating on identifying problems to become shaky and
had survived this far.

Her war was proving jolly interesting and eventful for 'Just a
ferry pilot.'
What a pity she was forbidden to share her latest exploits
with Max, Arabella, and Francis.   Now, with jet power, she
had seen the future of aviation and played a part in it too.

CHAPTER 28
MAX

Each evening when Max phoned Amber at her pool he was politely informed that she was not available being away on duty. So it was that he telephoned Arabella.

He introduced himself to his future mother-in-law and chatted fluently with her before sharing the good news that he had been granted five days leave to allow his marriage to take place. The date would give her three weeks to complete all the arrangements. They were both anxious to hear from Amber, and that her request for leave had been granted. Meanwhile he had forwarded his list of guests headed by his uncle, Sir Hubert Unsworth, Knight of the realm and general good egg. Eddy, who Max had designated as his best man, was still training, and instructing airmen for the RAF in Canada.   As they had been chums since boarding school, they both desperately hoped that Eddy would make it back in time.

If charm could be transmitted over the phone, then Max was your man! All his efforts raised in Arabella was more concern on top of her anxiety for her daughter's whereabouts. Perhaps she was being too fanciful in both cases.

As Max hopefully awaited a call from his missing fiancée he

eyed up the two letters on his desk.

He reasoned that the one bearing Uncle Hubert's crest would be unlikely to bring him comfort. The last one from his jovial patron had been scathing, in effect it had read-
Dear Max,
I know you young chaps fighting for dear old England need to let off steam when you can, but the last list of your bills on my account caused me to let off a good deal of steam. I don't mind you going up to London on a 24 hour, and as the bills always seem to be for two, I presume you are entertaining one of you Popsies! Good luck to you, and I do understand. Just can you go easy on the champagne and fine dining every time? You are making quite a dent in my income. I know you are my heir, my boy, but I do want there to be something left for you to inherit, and for me to enjoy the odd supper and brandy at my club.

Uncle Hubert

Since it failed to end with 'Your affectionate Uncle Hubert,' Max knew he was in his bad books.

By now his uncle must have received the accounts from the jewellers for Amber's engagement ring, together with a rather large bill from the Savoy. Gingerly he opened the envelope and took out the letter –

Dear Max,

Well done me boy.   You've bagged yourself an heiress!

When you first mentioned her, I knew the name, Amber Seymour, seemed familiar.   Her mother is the famous singer, Arabella Seymour, <u>but</u> she married Francis Grantley of the Grantley Industries Corporation.

Your affianced is their daughter.   She will not only inherit pots of money from her father, but also the Courtneys house and estate from her mother.

I'll stand all your wedding expenses, but after that MRS MAX can foot the bills.   A word of advice – drop all the popsies – it's not worth losing such a prize.

Your affectionate

Uncle Hubert

'Great heavens,' Max exclaimed out loud.   No wonder Amber had her own sports car, cottage, and beautiful clothes.   Now he understood why her flying grades were 'Exceptional.'   She had been flying since she was twelve with a devoted aunt.   No mention that she had been flying Grantley planes.   When had she intended to tell him? Obviously after their marriage.   Well, he'd really fallen on his feet, and must watch his behaviour and his alcohol input. Wouldn't do to drink too much at his wedding.   It would upset his new mother-in-law and incapacitate his performance with his new bride.

Happy days ahead indeed. All he had to do now was to stay alive when he led his squadron of Spits into battle.

H s second letter was pathetic and pleading. It was in an almost childish hand on cheap scented paper.

Dear Max,
I know I shouldn't write to you at your base, but I must let you know that I need to see you very soon.
You see, dear, I'm pregnant. You did say we'd be married so I let you go too far, and I think you got me a little tiddly. I've got a job behind the bar at The Lion. Please can you come over one evening so we can sort out what to do. I daren't tell my parents. They've always warned me about you men in uniform, but you know Max there has only – or can ever be you.

Your loving

Linda xxx

PS Please make it soon
From delight to despair within the space of two letters!

Max never doubted for a moment that the baby Linda was

carrying was his. She wasn't his usual 'Popsie' material. He had noticed her at the station dances because she never took her eyes off him. She only ever sipped a soft drink and was always simply dressed but was very pretty with large blue eyes and shining fair hair. At last, he had asked her to dance and found something touching in her unsophisticated adoration.

She would be overcome with shyness in a hotel, so he drove her into the country for a picnic. The mess had done him proud, and her eyes shone with happiness as she enjoyed the food.

He couldn't resist seducing her knowing that he was the first man to make love to her. He was surprisingly gentle and if she experienced any discomfort she hid her face in his chest. Afterwards she looked at him with such love and trust that he promised to take care of her always and in her innocence, she believed him.

Now he had won a far bigger prize. Once he had married Amber and had access to the allowance, he would consider his due, he would pay off Linda and make provision for her child. Then he was hit with the realisation; it was his child too. Sowing wild oats was one thing, but being responsible for a new life was another. Oh God – what was he to do?

Max drove to the Red Lion the next evening. There she was

gamely serving pints and trying to be cheerful for the customers. He could see that her face looked a little pinched and her eyes a little dull. Pregnancy was not being kind to her. The landlord gave her a fifteen-minute break to spend with her fellow. Linda was pathetically grateful to see him – sure in the knowledge that he would look after her.

Max held her hard and tried to break it gently.
'Linda dear I have to tell you that I've been seeing someone else. Before your letter arrived, I had proposed to her. We are to be married in three weeks' time. It's all arranged, and I can't back out.

I'll help you with money for yourself and the baby. Here's £50 to start with, then the same every month, and a much larger sum when he's born. If you want to stay at home, I'll help you rent somewhere.'

'I don't want your money, I want you' she burst out.

'Yes, you do, for the baby. Now take it please, Linda.'
She was too upset to go back to work behind the bar, so he ran her home. She waved to him despondently as he drove away. He suddenly longed to go back and tell her it would be fine, then suppressed the thought quickly. He was to be married and that must be the end of it.

CHAPTER 29
COURTNEYS HOSTS A WEDDING

With Amber's five day leave also confirmed, Bridie and Arabella had free rein to go ahead with their wedding plans. What had worked for Arabella and Francis was again put in place despite wartime restrictions and shortages.

The buffet tables would be set up in the Great Hall with the best table linens already washed and starched. Each dish was allocated its place and the great stone urns would again sport their cascades of foliage and flowers. Small tables would be placed in the shade of trees so guests could sit where they chose.

Arabella had hoped for a wedding cake from Fortnum and Mason, but had to settle for a local baker, given most of her food coupons. Neither could a London band be hired. She hoped that the dance band that played at all the local dances would fit the bill.

Bridie was satisfied that everything she could do in advance was ready.

Amber drove up in mid-afternoon. Her first sight of Courtneys left her quite emotional. All her life in America her mother had told her of the wonderful English home where she had been born. Not grand like Fairhaven, but old and golden, and with the sun glinting from its windows, it seemed to welcome her with all the warmth and comfort enjoyed by the generations before her.

When Arabella came to greet her, they embraced then stood together with arms linked.

'Oh Mom, it is absolutely magical. No wonder you love it so much and couldn't bear to leave here forever. I'm just so lucky to be married from Courtneys. I think I've fallen in love not just with Max, but with the house.'

'Come in darling. You'll want to freshen up, unpack, and look at all Bridie's preparations, and then I want to show you the rose garden.'

Amber might be a modern American girl wearing slacks and casual sweater, yet as she looked around, she felt a benediction fall on her.

It was as if the house had taken her to its heart, ready to offer her contentment and comfort. Had it always embraced the young women who had come here as brides, and nourished them as they had nourished generations of children, growing up safe within its sheltering walls? She felt their spirits looking down on her, their encouragement to join their ranks and their hopes for her future.

Arabella had stayed silent as Amber turned to her to try and express feelings.

'I know Amber, it is the same for all the Courtney women. This house will nurture you and care for you and your children. You are the next generation and must carry the torch forward. Now you are having to fight for liberty, as these women fought against illnesses and improvident husbands to maintain this house. You feel the past now and it will equip you to face the future.'

Her future lay here with Max. He would soon arrive to meet Arabella and Robert. They would have supper together and finalise all the arrangements for tomorrow's great day, before he left to spend the night with Christopher and Laura Richards, as Francis had done before his marriage to Arabella.

Amber knew she would miss her father greatly, but war separated so many families.

Max arrived very soon after Amber had changed into a very fetching blue dress and was there on the steps with Arabella to welcome her darling fiancé.

They dined simply, for the great feast would be on the morrow. Max was totally charming, in turns serious and then amusing and lighthearted. The conversation flowed easily until Arabella and Robert excused themselves, so as to leave the couple together.

As they embraced, Max was so enthusiastic.
'Won't be long now darling, and what a spiffing place to hold our reception. I called at the church on the way and had a word with the vicar. We'll have the most wonderful time, won't we?' As he kissed her ardently Amber agreed with shining eyes.

CHAPTER 30
BRIDIE

Miss Amber's wedding was debonair.   I'm not entirely sure what it means but with all those dashing RAF officers in their fancy uniforms and all Miss Amber's friends in their elegant A.T.A uniforms it looked like a Hollywood picture.

Then what do you think, could you ever believe it?   There's Max the bridegroom better than a blond Errol Flynn.   He'd knock your eyes out.

Miss Arabella was resplendent – there aren't I the one for big words.   Finest mother of the bride ever.

As for Miss Amber!
She's a pilot so she'd not want to turn out like the fairy on the Christmas tree.   It seemed she'd ordered her dress from Hollywood, and I believed it.   Sure, it was dead glamourous. If you think of Rita Hayworth, Lana Turner or your favourite actress, Miss Amber would have outshone them.   It's her hair really, and the way in which she carries herself which gives her presence.

Her dress was a sort of ivory crepe dinner dress with a bolero.   All around the edges were tiny seed pearls.   No veil, but a padded head band with pearls again.   With a simple spray of orchids, she looked the bees' knees.

I'm saving the best bit till last, because just as the bridegroom arrived, a motor bike roared up to the church. The chap jumped off and shed his jacket and helmet. When he turned around – you'll never guess – it was the BEST MAN. For me, the best ever 'cos it was my Eddy who I thought was in Canada – and here he was at the village church.

He dashed over, gave me a kiss, and bolted into church to take up his position before the bride arrived. I hoped that Max hadn't forgotten to hand him the ring.

Well, Miss Amber even promised to obey him as they took their vows, which I know she never will. She's too high spirited and rich, but he'll find out soon enough. They left the church with the organ ringing in their ears and the church bells to add to the din. Showers of confetti, and all the usual hubbub sent them on their way back to Courtneys.

I wanted to find my Eddy, but there he was in the centre of a group of RAF chaps. Then they turned to get to their cars I darted in before the A.T.A. girls got to him.
My he really is beautiful, not just handsome, with his dark curly hair and flashing blue eyes. Of course he's got the charm of the Irish from me!
I'm away to the reception and leave him to his fate.

CHAPTER 31
THE BRIDE 1943

The congregation rose to their feet, smiling as Robert escorted her down the aisle of St. Barts.

The vicar's sonorous voice reached every corner of the church.

'Will you take this woman, Amber, Aurora, Dorothea, Evelyn Grantley to be your lawful wedded wife?'

A small ripple ran around the congregation. How had the Amber Seymour they knew morphed into Amber Grantley, one of the Grantleys? Now as she made her vows, she became Amber Dickinson.

Her eyes were downcast as she looked at the platinum wedding band Max was placing on her finger.

As she raised them to him, she somehow looked beyond him. In that instant she knew she was marrying the wrong man! Here was the grown-up version of the curly-haired, merry-eyed mischievous boy in the Hoppner painting which hung over the bed where she had slept last night and would be occupying tonight as Max's bride. She must surely be the young girl making daisy chains. The man standing at Max's side had black curly hair and vivid eyes. He gazed at her in stunned recognition.

'Concentrate, concentrate' Amber admonished herself. You can't flee, it's too late, smile, look joyous, gaze at your husband, wave gaily. Your mother is an actress, and you must give the performance of your life.

Pray heaven he doesn't kiss the bride. She'll either return his kiss or faint. She could only hope that the photographs would not show her disquiet.

Their guests were waiting to cheer the bride and groom at Courtneys. She found herself shaking hands, greeting people she had never met before and accepting their compliments and kisses.

Max introduced his Uncle Hubert to her,
'Enchanted my dear, delighted to welcome you into the family. You'll soon knock us into shape. Max is a jolly lucky chap.'

He moved on to shower everyone with his bonhomie. All were 'my boy,' 'my dear chap,' 'dear girl,' or 'dear lady', accompanied by a firm handshake or an admiring look and compliment.

Drinks were being served and enthusiastically enjoyed. Beer was still the chosen tipple of all the RAF officers.

Champagne and wine were for toasts.

The buffet was greeted with delight and a level of disbelief. Where had all this wonderful food come from?

Uncle Hubert was most impressed.
'Up to the highest standards of any society wedding dear lady,' he said to Arabella. 'Don't know how you've managed it, but jolly well done.'

Arabella flushed with pleasure as his words were obviously sincere.

The cake was cut, the speeches made, the toasts drunk and as the guests drifted around the gardens the great hall was set up for dancing.

Amber had feared that the RAF contingent would become a bit rowdy. She had experienced this in many messes. Instead, the guests worked off their energies on the dance floor and appeared lively but not drunk. They must have an inexhaustible thirst for beer and could certainly hold their drink.

At last Uncle Hubert took his leave, waving from the back of a stately Rolls Royce. No problem with petrol supplies there! Every guest agreed that Max and Amber's wedding had been a huge success, no bride more beautiful, no bridegroom more handsome. Every morsel of food was more delicious consumed in Courtneys' flower filled rooms and gardens.

Arabella and Robert had moved to the Dower House, so as to leave Courtneys to the newlyweds. Amber kissed her mother tenderly with a full heart for all her love and kindness. She was a little puzzled as to why her mother had referred to her as a 'Courtney' bride probably because Amber had been born here.

Soon it was time for Max to take her to bed to consummate their marriage. Here she was, a bride at last, after a most glorious English day to bless her wedding and their future. She supposed GOLDEN described it, and so it would be remembered.

Why then was the only thing she really wanted to remember was Eddy? People had laughed at his witty speech. He had known Max since they had met at boarding school aged 8. They had competed fiercely both at sport and academically. They had developed an enduring friendship of great depth and mutual regard which had matured and endured.

Amber had not heard a word of it, lost in a confusion of emotions. Max must never guess. She could not play him false and disrupt their trust in each other, yet when she had danced with Eddy it had been a slow foxtrot. He had held her lightly, but nothing could prevent the charge of electricity, the recognition that they had been meant for each other. The faint remembrance from their earliest days at Courtneys when he had romped with Flossy the dog, and Wing the new black foal.

She had remembered Wing and had called every one of her ponies and horses Wing. Why had she forgotten Eddy who had always stayed near her in the garden? Why must he come back into her life on the very day that she married another man?

She prepared to welcome her husband. Teeth and hair brushed, faint lipstick and perfume, the finest silk nightdress, and a bleak heart. Not the greatest combination, but Max loved her and deserved a willing and equally loving reception.

Amber had certainly taken Max's advice to be prepared. She had no intention of having a child until this war was over. The A.T.A. needed all its pilots for ferry duties. Motherhood must wait.

First the act of procreation must take place as a rehearsal for the real thing. She pushed such thoughts aside and smiled a welcome to her new husband.

'Alone at last, what a day it's been, Amber. We have so

much to thank your Mother, Robert and Bridie for. Now come and kiss me darling. We must make the most of every minute together.'

His kisses as always were wonderful, full of love and now real desire for his beautiful bride. His habitual techniques took over. It was rather like flying his Spitfire. Switches turned on, buttons pressed, propeller spun, engine fire and boosted. Then away they would soar up into the blue beyond until he fired his rockets and then WOW!

Sadly, Max's scenario came to a juddering halt. His engine fired, but then cut out with a whimper. His next attempt at a restart was no more successful.
"I'm so sorry darling" he said ruefully. How could this be happening? He had no trouble at all to satisfy any of his Popsies. Why did this splendid girl with her athletic figure, firm breasts and self-confidence render him ineffectual? Were they just physically incompatible? Had they mistaken an immediate and strong attraction for the real thing?

Amber was not alone in realising her mistake. Max suddenly longed for the quiet adoration of the soft and clinging Linda. He would forever be her hero. She would have clung to him and soothed him and placed his hand to feel where their child lay. Why had he been such a coward? Amber would have understood when he confessed and would have released him from their engagement.

Some Battle of Britain hero, some air ace, leader of men.   He was nothing but a coward.

Amber sensed his pain and humiliation.   She stroked his shoulders and said
'It doesn't matter.   Let's just cuddle up and go to sleep.'   So, they did just that, locked in thoughts of other people.

CHAPTER 32
EDDY

Eddy cut a swathe through all the women he met. It was rather like flying. The clear blue sky meant easy going, easily conquered girls with happy go lucky temperaments, out for a good time with a handsome officer.

Fluffy white clouds which wafted across the heavens were a little more difficult to catch. The dark storm clouds which made navigations so much harder yet so much more exciting required constant attention, flattery, and a safe landing.

Eddy was not knowingly promiscuous, restricting himself to one romance at a time. Yet temptation was seldom far away, and he was a red-blooded young man. He was involved in a war where life expectancy was limited, to say the least.

Somehow, he always knew that on Cloud 9 there waited a special girl, if only he could soar high enough to claim her.

It was cruel that when he did find her, alongside her stood a man in RAF uniform who turned out to be his own best friend.

Fate had been kind to Eddy, thus far. He had survived being shot up regularly during the Battle of Britain, running out of fuel, or engine failure, and was still here. The 'rest cure' of training new pilots in Canada had proved hair-raising at times, as they ignored instructions and flew dangerously. He had survived it all.

Now why had fate turned on him?
As soon as he had set eyes on Amber he knew that she was his Cloud 9 ideal girl. Their look of recognition and the closeness of their dance established that fact.

Eddy was due to report to Fighter Command HQ at Bentley Priory. He must spend the next morning with Bridie, who doted on her only child. She would be full of the wedding of course. Perhaps she would take the morning off from Courtneys and go out for a spin on the bike with him.

He would be duty bound to say goodbye to Max and hoped that if his Cloud 9 girl was there, he would not betray himself.

He managed it with a firm handshake for Max and a quick peck on the cheek for Amber.

'Cheerio then, I'll be seeing you,' and off he roared on his motorbike.
Did he guess that Amber rode pillion with her hands tightly clasped around him?
In her dreams!

CHAPTER 33
BACK TO BASE

The war was not about to stop for a wedding.   There were certainly changes.

Air Vice-Marshall Arthur Harris had taken control of Bomber Command in 1942.   The squadrons of Lancasters flew their raids on German cities night after night.   The heavy ack-ack defences and German Fighters took their toll.   With each plane lost went its crew of seven young men, lost in battle but forever comrades.

The 8th American Army Air Force flew the daylight raids with their huge B17 and B24 Flying Fortresses and Mustang Fighter escorts.

Every Lancaster lost or too severely damaged needed a replacement flown in from the factories in Manchester.   The A.T.A. were always busy.   Amber was used as an 'Observation pilot,' often given a new upgraded Mark to fly and report on, but did not test fly again.   She was glad to be back at her pool, enjoying the camaraderie of her fellows. There were always yarns in the mess, with near misses, and some U.S. - useless old crocks - to be reported on.

The ever-observant A.T.A. men and women could not fail to notice the build-up of gliders, and newly painted aircraft with different livery.   The second front must come next year.

Meanwhile just get on with your chits, fly what they gave you and hope that the forthcoming Autumn and Winter weather be fairly settled.

Uncle Hubert had written to Amber. Her mother had forwarded it from Courtneys.

'Now m'dear I've written to thank you mother for the splendid hospitality for your and Max's wedding. It really is time to make some return, so I want to invite you to come to me for Christmas. Surely, you'll get a few days leave? Not so sure about Max. I'm an old man and would like some young company. I'd like to show you around BROADGATES. It's not as grand as Courtneys, but it will belong to Max and you and your children. I like the cut of your jib. You'll have a good business brain, and these estates will need to be properly managed.

Your lovely mother and Robert would be very welcome too. Let me know nearer the time what you can manage. Cook is not a bad old girl, and the wine cellar is certainly worth sampling.

Your affectionate
Uncle Hubert'

'Oh gosh' thought Amber. 'Max, me, and our children to inherit! If only he knew that children would have to wait until after the war – and even then would probably never appear!'

To her total astonishment Arabella and Robert welcomed the idea. It would allow Bridie and the staff to have their own relaxed holiday, after all the efforts for Amber's wedding. So, both she and Arabella wrote to Uncle Hubert, and said they would be delighted to accept his invitation – RAF, A.T.A, Robert's hospital and Arabella's wireless programme permitting.

Arabella was thankful that she had abandoned her idea of asking Francis to investigate Max and his past. He was very obviously a war hero, and inspiration to his men, and seemed to be genuinely in love with Amber. As heir to a well-to-do and doting uncle, he didn't need Amber's money either.
It would be such a change to visit Broadgates and get to know its jovial owner.

CHAPTER 34
MAX 1943

As Max returned to his duties something had changed in him forever. He felt a Judas. He had denied Linda the right of his protection, and his name. What would she put on the child's birth certificate where the father should be named? Plus, he had married Amber under false pretences with the disastrous result of his impotence. What a mess.

He must visit the Red Lion and give Linda more money. Instead of wanting to forget her and the whole business of her pregnancy, he wanted to know her plans and how he could best help her.

When Max strode into the Red Lion Linda was not behind the bar. He asked the landlord –
'I'd like to speak to Linda. Is she working tonight?'
'Fraid not. She went off sick last week if you get my meaning.'
Resisting the temptation to punch him, Max requested Linda's home address. He had dropped her at the end of her street before, but she had refused to allow him to drive up to her door because
" Mum wouldn't like it"

The door to the neat villa at No. 26 was answered by a middle-aged woman with faded fair hair, faded blue eyes and wearing a faded apron.

'I'd like to speak to Linda please. It is important.'

'Yes, and so would I. We had words last week. She packed her case and walked out. I suppose you'll know all about the reason. A bit late to come round now. If you find her, tell her I've calmed down and want her safe back home. I'll expect you to do the right thing by her.'

'You can be sure of that,' Max said as he handed her his phone number.

'Get her to ring me or leave a message – you too anytime.'

The next dance was due to be held at the weekend, so she'd surely come with a girlfriend. Then he'd be able to reassure her. This would be the last dance here. The nearby American base offered glamourous guys in slick uniforms with their movie star accents. A girl could do worse than fetch up in America, and there was always the lure of silk stockings and candy.

Max grew more and more anxious. Where was Linda and was she caring for the baby she was carrying? It was eating away at him because his almost casual seduction had led to her problems. She was a shy decent girl who had the misfortune to fall forever in love with Max. It wasn't just his good looks and the appeal of a uniform during wartime. She had seen through his shield of confidence to understand his responsibilities were draining his strength. He and Eddy had joined the RAF together. They both had learned to fly with the University Air Training Corps. All too soon they were both fast-tracked to satisfy the insatiable demand for Spitfire pilots. Somehow by skill or good luck they had survived the Battle of Britain. Max was, after a few years of war, too young to be a Squadron Leader, yet he assumed his responsibilities to great effect.

He was good at admin and was held in high regard and huge respect by his men. Where he led, they followed and fought long and hard to overcome their Luftwaffe foes. Max had revelled in their company and high regard. Now he felt that he had feet of clay. He slept fitfully, ate sparingly and sometimes felt a little light-headed and dizzy.

His squadron had just been re-equipped with Spitfire MK XIV's powered by the 2000 h.p RR GRIFFON engine. Though more powerful than the older planes, they were also more difficult to handle. He had led his squadron on many training flights, and now sorties over France, in preparation for the invasion which all knew would take place next year. None of them could miss the heightened activities at the American bases close by, nor the new camps being prepared for the incoming G.I.s. Soon they would be training in Southern England and the immortal phrase 'GOT ANY GUM CHUM?' would be heard as the English kids pursued an American truck – and the English girls pursued the G.I.s.

Max had read the orders of the day. He felt tired, so must

really grab a coffee and force down some toast.   The new planes were to fly over to France, to test the air defences and pinpoint any new radar stations.

On their return his wingman reported that Max's plane had landed heavily, bounced, and then settled back down.   It was most unlike the normal immaculate landings of his Squadron Leader.
'Just a bit off chaps.   Came in a bit too fast.   Watch, learn and have a care.'

The debrief showed that opposition was muted, and the pilots were indeed finding the plane harder to handle, but with its extra speed and fire power it would be formidable. Max took off smoothly and steadily.   No one would ever suspect by his demeanour and skill that he might as well be flying on empty fuel tanks.
For he had received a phone caller leaving a message. Strangely it was set out in formal tones –
'Regret to inform you that, following the discovery of her suitcase, the body of Miss Linda Walsh was discovered in the River Stour.   An inquest will be held into her death.'

So here he was, respected RAF officer and air ace, husband, nephew, lover, and father to a child who would now never be born.

Now he could add moral coward, deceiver, and yes

murderer. His self-loathing was overwhelming. How could he have been so blind and cruel in his response to Linda's despair, when he had repudiated her? What future could he have with Amber, when he nursed the knowledge of the deaths he had caused? Max felt sick with his own despair.

He casually chased off a ME 109 with a turn of speed and a burst of heavy fire which the German pilot had not expected.

He gave no sign of his inner demons as his men heard over their intercoms –
'OK chaps, let's get back to base for some bacon and eggs.'

It was then he saw her, reaching out beseechingly from a cloud.

His wingman heard only a groan, then saw Max slumped over the controls as the Spitfire plunged into the channel. No attempt was made to open the canopy.

Pilot Officer Campbell took over command. They flew in a circle to check, but there was no debris and so sign of

MAXIMILLIAN HUBERTUS DICKINSON

Because he had engaged the 109, Max's death was entered as 'Lost in Action.'

A brief service would be held for him at the base, as it had for so many brave airmen.

He would be replaced, and soon enough any memory would fade.

CHAPTER 35

The telegram awaited Amber in the CO's office as the Anson 'taxi' returned her after a full day of chits.   She was looking forward to driving back to the cottage, a leisurely bath and supper with Honor.   Then perhaps a few chapters of 'The History of Britain.'

Perhaps Max would phone tonight.   He had sounded a little weary three nights ago.

They had seen each other so rarely since their wedding.   Her days off never coincided with his.   The last time they had been together was when she had delivered one of the latest Spitfires to his base.   She had found it challenging to fly, but did not doubt it would prove to be a formidable fighting force.   Honor had really disliked hers and regretted losing the simpler 'glove fitting' earlier models.

Max had greeted her so happily with a strong hug and a stunning series of kisses.   Never mind the onlookers.   A chap was surely entitled to give his wife a kiss and a cuddle after so many weeks apart.   They had such a short time together before the Anson arrived to collect her.

'I'll leave you to read it alone.   Come out when you feel ready.   You'll need tea and toast, so I'll send some in to you.' So as her mother had done so many times in the past Amber drank her tea, nibbled her toast, and absorbed the fact that she was now a widow.

Life did have a way of rearing up and biting you in the bum. Today it had really sunk its teeth into her. Dry eyed, she thanked her CO who offered her condolences, then asked her if she would like a few days of compassionate leave.

'Just two please. Then I'd like to get back to flying. It is the best tribute I can pay to my husband.'
'Agreed,' said her CO who was a man of few words but who used his officers with maximum efficiency. He greatly valued the only one to be labelled both Exceptional and Outstanding.

Honor was brilliant to Amber. She allowed her friend to share her sadness and regrets without interruption until their supper arrived. Neither were hungry, for the day's emotions had taken their toll.

Amber felt able to telephone Arabella with the dire news. It was not ambivalent. No 'Missing in Action' just the bleak 'Died in Action.'

'Would Arabella be at home next day? Could Amber drive over to spend the day and stay the night?'

'Of course,' replied Arabella. 'You know Robert and I will

help wherever we can. Can you bear to ring Hubert? He will be devasted and since he knows you both loved Max he'll want to speak to you.'

'Will do, and will you please tell Bridie? I'll be there about 2.30pm. Don't bother about lunch. Let's have a cup of tea together, and then supper with Robert.'

How easy it was to deal with mundane details following a death. She supposed that the base would hold some sort of short service for Max that she would need to attend. They all flew day after day facing mechanical and weather problems without flinching, and never expecting to die. Yet many ATA pilots had died on duty.

For Max and his fellow pilots and their frequent encounters with the enemy the risks were so much higher, and now Max had perished.

The enormity of it hit home when she telephoned Uncle Hubert. The dear man seemed to have collapsed like a burst balloon. All he could repeat was
'Not Max, not my golden boy. No, not Max.'
'Oh, Hubert it's too terrible, but we have no choice but to bear it. Max was so brave, and he died fighting for his country. I'm just clinging on to that.'
'Quite right m'dear, quite right. He was a proper patriot.'

Then he broke into noisy sobs followed by profuse apologies.

'I'll come and see you as soon as I can, and I'll bring Mom. When she sings for you, then you'll feel better.   And we'll remember Max always.'

That seemed to calm Hubert, and they said 'Goodnight.'

Amber knew his grief was much deeper than hers.   She had dreaded the call which she knew must follow.

It was indeed Eddy on the line.   To her huge relief he was fully in control of himself.   He offered his condolences in the traditional British stiff upper lip style.
'When we meet, we'll talk about Max shall we?   He's been my friend forever, and you've lost your husband.   We'll help each other.   Goodnight now Amber.'
'Goodnight Eddy and thank you.'

They rang off.   Too much unsaid.

CHAPTER 36
AMBER

As soon as she saw Courtneys and her mother, Amber felt so much better. A hug, a fond kiss and then tea and whiskey cake in the library.

Amber sat on the rug at Arabella's feet. Arabella stroked her child's hair.
'You know your father refurbished this room for me. I'll never forget when he unlocked the door and brought me in. There was the great Audubon Book of American Birds where it had always been.' (Careful Arabella! She had nearly said 'Before your real father, Richard Courtney, vandalised it.)
'It's in a bank vault for the duration of the war, but it will surely be back.'

'I've spoken to Francis, and he'll telephone now you are here. It's all so beastly and unfair, and it's happening to so many families.'

'Will you tell me about the books Mama, and those that were Sir Edward's favourites. I'm enjoying British history and there may be some very old and unusual volumes?'

Arabella recognised a welcome change of subject, and they spent some pleasant hours examining books and folios before Robert arrived back. He immediately drew Amber into his arms for a comforting hug. His sadness for her was heartfelt. He had shared the unenviable news of death with so many of his patients' relatives and knew the words of comfort which helped most. The three of them ate dinner informally in the library.

Thankfully, Amber had been given a different room from the one where she had spent her wedding night with Max.

She had remembered her mother's chosen Courtneys dress and wore a long black skirt, cream blouse, and wide red belt. Life must hold some colour surely.

Bridie had unpacked for her and left a letter expressing her sadness on Max's death.
Amber knew the words hid relief that Eddy was still safe. It was human nature after all. They had clasped hands and kissed downstairs, their eyes expressing their emotions.

Amber was able to eat some of the delicious soup, and the lightest omelette with salad, followed by a cup of real coffee. Robert knew that if Amber could have a good night's sleep, she would start her recovery.

Later, after dinner Francis called, and she was thrilled to talk to her father even under such sad circumstances. He had never known Max but would surely have liked him and welcomed him into the Grantley family. His sympathy touched Amber so much.

He assured her that all was well at Fairhaven, with Lucinda, Johnnie, and her aunts. 'It won't be long now before the war is won darling.'
'I know Pops. I'm so glad I came over here but oh I do miss you so.'

If only she knew, thought Francis, how bleak he found life without her buoyant energy and love. He was certain that the invasion of Europe would be launched from England next summer. The might of American support was already turning the war in Europe in the Allies' favour. American Forces were finding the Japanese determined enemies. The war in the Pacific was proving a long hard slog.

Meanwhile, Francis was becoming wealthier by the day as his company poured out the weaponry that the war demanded. He just longed for it to end. Then he could take Lucinda on a long extravagant holiday and try to restore their marriage. Now he felt just too tired.

What a fantastic daughter Arabella had given him. Would she sing her lullabies to the children which Amber would surely bear in the future when she re-married? Now he was getting ahead of himself!

They ended their phone call with her usual – 'love you lots

Pops. Please take care of yourself. Life is so precious, isn't it?' With the smallest of sobs, and as he sent his love, she cut the connection.

Then she made her 'Goodnights' to Robert and Arabella and retired to bed.

Amber's return to her A.T.A. pool was uneventful. She was greeted with an understanding nod or a quiet 'Sorry.' The sheer routine kicked in and kept her steady …..You visited meteorology, collected your chits for the day, heard a few suppressed moans about their contents. Then it was on to your pool driver, or the arrival of the Anson taxi plane to be delivered for the first flight of the day.

They were all flying most of the time. Only bad weather restricted their movements. The number and variety of the planes she ferried often surprised Amber. All the A.T.A. pilots must have been saving the RAF countless hours in the air.

As always, Amber concentrated totally during each flight, then tried to relax during the short breaks at each of the bases she visited. She met many interesting people on the days when she was grounded by poor weather. Keeping busy stopped her thinking about Max, his death, and their short-lived marriage. There were always new and modified aircraft to fly, with the promise of even more in the New

Year.   1944 must surely bring the invasion of Europe.

Christmas was upon them.   For their Christmas visit
Arabella, Amber and Robert arrived at the Manor to be
warmly welcomed by Sir Hubert.   He had lost some of his
ebullience but was clearly delighted to see them.
They settled in and then gathered to enjoy coffee with a nip
of brandy for the men, and home-made delicious shortbread
biscuits.

Sir Hubert had asked them to accompany him to Church and
had requested that Amber wear her A.T.A. uniform.   Since
no one had met Max's wife it would help them to identify
her.

The Vicar greeted them, and the Churchwarden led them to
the family pew.   When the organist finished his intro, the
Vicar gave his formal welcome then announced –
'We are here to honour the memory of Squadron Leader
Max Dickinson.   Many of you have known him since he came
to live with his uncle, Sir Hubert, as a young boy.   He
developed into a splendid young man.   When Britain was
besieged by war, he become a fine officer who gave his life in
fighting for the country he loved. Two fellow officers are
here to represent his squadron.   We welcome them among
us.
I now invite Group Captain Brydson to make a presentation
to Mrs. Amber Dickinson.'

Amber moved forward to stand alongside the Group Captain.

'I am commanded by His Majesty the King to present to you this medal awarded posthumously to Squadron Leader Max Dickinson for outstanding gallantry.'

The Distinguished Flying Cross was presented to Amber. They turned together to bow to the altar in Max's memory.

The second officer placed a plaque bearing Max's name, rank, and date of death on the WW1 memorial in the chapel. He saluted it smartly, and then both officers marched from the church.   The short memorial service ended as prayers were said, which gave them all a great deal of comfort.

When the full service concluded, they shared tea and warm mince pies with the rest of the congregation before returning to the Manor in Sir Hubert's chauffeur driven Rolls Royce. The driver was an ancient retainer who took pride in his vehicle and drove at a stately pace.
Amber handed the medal to Sir Hubert, who glowed with pride, and then deep sadness for his lost nephew.   How very cruel war is. Amber wanted to rage against the waste of it all, but wisely held her tongue.

After this their Christmas passed quietly yet was surprisingly comforting.   Uncle Hubert was as good as his word.   Cook proved to be a very capable 'Old Girl,' and the two maids kept everything orderly with warm fires and frequent hot drinks for the visitors.

Although the corridors were draughty, the reception rooms and bedrooms were cosy. Amber was at last able to relax, slept better and enjoyed the food. Cook had been grateful for the Courtneys hamper of game and vegetables. Tactfully Bridie had not included any desserts or cakes, which might have impugned Mrs. Harman's capabilities.

The gift of good claret and port delighted Uncle Hubert, while the fine Cuban cigars from Amber were judged an extreme luxury.

Robert and Hubert found much in common, while Arabella adored browsing through Hubert's extensive library. Amber stuck to brisk walks and reading British history to distract her troubled thoughts.

The after-dinner cigar smoke became little overwhelming until Arabella protested and aired the room.

Then she sang for Hubert, her husband, and her daughter. When she ended with 'Silent Night' Sir Hubert shed a tear, while Amber gulped back hers.

When the small party left, they knew that firm friendships had been made which would surely endure.

CHAPTER 37
1944

Amber returned to duty at the A.T.A. pool. January 1944 saw them busier than ever as the buildup to the invasion of Europe gathered force. The ferry team needed to fly with ever more care as there was so much aerial activity.

Amber's chits regularly included the very fast and light Mosquito, so valuable to the RAF on reconnaissance and precision bombing raids.

She flew and reported on the sleek Hawker Typhoon, which would replace that old warhorse, the Hurricane. The many days of flying, interspersed with the occasional days off, helped her to slowly recover from her whirlwind marriage and its tragic aftermath.

She wondered constantly about Eddy, but he did not telephone. In fact, she learned what he was doing from Bridie, on the rare days when she could visit Courtneys. There the springtime was especially beautiful. The many bulbs which Maggie Jones had planted, especially the drifts of snowdrops close to the house, were wonderful in their beauty.

It was hard to believe that war was raging over the whole of Europe.

Back at base there was only one chit, issued by the CO in person.

'Another special report, Officer Dickinson. You've read all the info sheets? It does have a reputation of being tricky to fly. The counter-spin propellers are unusual, and it is heavy on the controls. If you are at all uneasy, put down asap.'

'Yes sir,' said Amber and made her visit to the meteorological office.

'Nothing much to worry you, just a spot of low cloud. You'll soon be above it and then it will soon clear.'

With her night bag and parachute, Amber set off for her departure field. The plane awaited her, fuelled up and sleek. What a stunning looking kite. With her 'bible notes' at a glance on her knee, she went through the A.T.A. test routine. Satisfied, she was given the thumbs up from the ground crew and took off without fuss. The details of the special flight instrument she was due to test had been handed to her to study the previous day.

She was to reach a certain landmark, then return to base to make her report. Amber climbed to her usual cruising height, maintaining her course. Within seconds she had exchanged cloud for dense fog – all-enveloping and totally disorientating. The A.T.A. instruction was to put down at the nearest available airstrip, but that was miles away and she would be unable to see it in any case.

From the earliest days of aviation man had reached for the skies with their puny aircraft. They held the conviction that they would succeed in leaving their earthbound existence yet would return safely. Time and again they failed, yet others strode into their shoes and carried on the fight ONWARDS AND UPWARDS. The elements would swat them down yet still they flew.
Soon bullets and rockets and shells were thrown at them by other men and machines and would send them spiralling to earth. Yet still they flew, intrepid and determined.

Amber numbered herself and the earlier women pioneers among them. Was flying a sort of disease, a compulsion too hard to resist?

Enveloped in the dense fog and totally disorientated, her life was in the balance. Only skill and good luck could save her.

The luck came as the merest break in the bank of fog. Far ahead was a patch of green. Unhesitatingly she cut her engines, her mind fixed on where she must aim for. She lowered the landing gear and only pulled out of the descent when her altimeter warned her how low she was.

The ground came up to hit her with some force as she

slammed the brakes to full, completely blind to what lay ahead.

Her plane veered by 30 degrees and stopped so smartly that despite her restraining harness she jerked forward before banging her head on the back of seat on the recoil.

Amber extricated herself from the seatbelt, opened the canopy and dragged herself out onto the wing. She slipped untidily onto the grass. It was essential that she checked for visible damage and if there was a fuel leak scooted fast. All she could do was fumble around the plane peering unhappily through the fog. Then she blacked out and collapsed to the ground.

A warm wet tongue was licking her face as Amber came to. She opened her eyes and prepared to push this unwelcome attention away. She looked into the bright intelligent face of a foxy little dog, who looked gravely back at her.

'That's enough Jenny love, she's awake now. Can you sit up, miss, if I support you?'
Amber nodded as he turned into the fog and called
'Quiet Bessie, that's enough' to a dog who was barking vigorously out of their sight.
'We'll get you up and to the house into the warm, you're shaking like mad, an' no wonder.'
'No, I must stay with the plane and keep it safe.'

'Never fear miss, Jim and Alfie have brought rifles. We're all in the Home Guard. They'll stand guard with Bessie. She'd drive away the devil himself. Let's get you in and we'll phone the police to let your base know what's happened. Jenny'll know the way. She can smell the kitchen from a mile off. Look lively lads and fire off a couple of rounds if you need old Denis to send re-enforcements.'

'With an arm around her waist and hers around his stout shoulders they limped over the grass, through a paddock and stable yard. Then he threw open a door and in a stentorian voice shouted
'Anybody in, we need some help here?'
'Oh, tis you a-bellowin. George! Who've you got there out in this fog?'
Then catching sight of his charge
'Why Miss Amber! No questions now, help me with her George. It's to bed you'll go young lady and no objections either. JOAN, VIOLET where the divil are ye at? Let's be getting Miss Amber into bed with hot water bottles for she's suffering with shock.
Joan, blow the blasted whistle for John Webster, can't you?'

With Bridie in full sail, all was smartly accomplished. Dr Robert was phoned for from the hospital.
'Don't care if he drives wi' torches in front, we need him fast.'

Amber sank into oblivion in the comfort of soft warm sheets and feather pillows.   A quietly insistent voice broke into her clouded brain.

'Amber, Amber, I need you to wake up and answer me.

Did you hit your head?	NOD
Does it hurt?	NO
Have you vomited?	NO

Follow my finger'

Slowly Robert checked that her movements were all in working order.

At last, she was given sips of a warm drink and was about to snuggle down under the covers in her warm winceyette nightgown.

Suddenly Amber struggled upright.

'My plane, have you rung my pool?'

'All done,' said Bridie.

'I found the number on Miss Arabella's desk.   I've rung Eddy too; sure, he'll want to know.   They're sending a ground crew and pilot along.   You're not to worry.'

'George and the Home Guard are saving it from German spies – even if there are any they'll be lost in this fog, and Bessy will be up and at em in a flash.'

Bridie looked down at her anxiously.

'Your mother 'll be back from London as soon as she can get a train.   No fretting now, off to sleep with you, and when you wake cook 'll have something special for you.'

Amber heard Bridie question Robert as they left the room. 'She's taken a nasty knock on the back of her head, from the seat I think. Probably the recoil from her landing. Her helmet and the thick pleat of her hair will have cushioned the blow. Someone should sit with her in case she vomits. If she does, call me at once. I'll be in the library, and I'll check on her every hour.'

How was it even believable that Amber had landed on Courtney land, and in such terrible conditions? Why had she even been flying at all?

Bridie had been calling down curses on whoever had sent Amber up to risk her life. It was surely a miracle from the Holy Mother that she had crashed at Courtneys of all places, where she would have the greatest care, or her name wasn't Bridie Quinlan!

Robert lit the fire, accepted Bridie's tray of tea and cake gratefully, and worried, about Arabella trying to make her way back in this abominable fog.

All his experience told him that Amber was suffering from bruising and shock. She was a fit active young woman. Her blood pressure was on the low side, but she should soon recover. He dared not even think of an alternative scenario, or how he could have faced Arabella.   Amber had survived a serious forced landing using all the skills and experience still available to her, and Arabella would know how best to nurse and encourage her daughter's recovery.   She would have felt so helpless if Amber had been flying in America.

When Arabella returned, he held her close and then told her all that he knew of Amber's crash and her present condition. She and Bridie took turns to sit with Amber all night.   They listened for any change in her breathing, gave her drinks of water, and Arabella prayed for her daughter as she had never prayed before.   Across the Atlantic Francis was doing the same.

Thankfully, Amber awoke in good form grateful for the good fortune which had saved her, and the part that Courtneys had played in her rescue.   She felt such a mixture of emotions.   Shock at her forced landing, amazement that she had survived it, and a supreme gratitude that God had given her a second chance at life.
She had washed, brushed her hair, and was sitting up expectantly in bed for Bridie to deliver her breakfast.   There was a tap on the door which swung open to reveal not Bridie, but Eddy.

He knelt at her bedside, took her hand, and kissed it.   As he looked up at her make-up free face, lovely hair, and unfashionable nightdress, he thought she had never looked more beautiful.

Because she was ALIVE.
By some miracle, his Cloud 9 girl was still on this earth and not dashed to pieces in the remains of her plane.

Then he saw the painting of the two children hanging over Amber's bed.
'Amber that's you and me,' he exclaimed.
'No Eddy, it was painted years and years before we were even born; yet the artist might have had us for models.   The boy especially is so well painted.   He has your merry eyes and air of mischief.   But why are you here?'

Eddy explained that he had been sent from Fighter Command HQ to salvage the secret instrument which Amer had been testing.   Was she able to report?

Amber sat very upright –
'The meteorology report gave light cloud – no mention of fog.   Suddenly I was enveloped in thick glutinous fog, and completely disorientated.
There was no time to read the required height and activate the device I was due to test.   On seeing a green stretch ahead through a break in the fog, I decided to put down. With zero visibility I landed heavily and regret the damage caused to the aircraft.
This is a new experience for me, and I apologise for not

completing my mission.'

With that, Amber fell back onto her pillows and burst into tears of frustration at her fall from grace.

'Don't cry darling. I'll retrieve the wretched thing and someone else can have a go in proper weather conditions. Shush darling now let me leave with a smile and a proper kiss. Then just concentrate on getting better.'

She hugged the memory of their kiss, and he had called her darling – twice!

He left her to assess the plane with the engineers. It was too damaged to fly and was removed on a RAF low loader.

Neither did Eddy return but began to telephone her whenever he could.

The build up to the allied invasion was in full swing. There was constant air activity above Courtneys. Amber now sat in the garden and sought out the planes overhead using Robert's binoculars. How she longed to be airborne again.

Her mother cosseted her and begged her to take time to recuperate.

Robert declined to sign her off to return to her pool, where an A.T.A. doctor would examine her.   Amber's low blood pressure still concerned him.

For Arabella, the comparison of Amber's head injury reminded her too closely of Richard Courtney's fall, apparent recovery, then sudden death.   Surely Amber would not follow where her real father had led?

The secrecy of Amber's true birth father was bearing heavily on her mother.   Still, she kept the secret.

It was the noise which woke the household.   The sky was dark with wave after wave of troop-carrying gliders, Mosquitos, Spitfires and American Lightnings – some to disgorge their paratroopers, and others to protect the beach landings.

Amber chafed at her inactivity and longed to be back at her pool.   A.T.A. activity had been restricted for several days as there were too many military flights.

Eddy had not phoned her for several days.   She knew that the RAF would have a policy of establishing forward bases in France to support the ground forces' advance, and she suspected that Eddy would be involved in this work.

She was able to speak to Francis and allay her father's fears.

'I'm fine Pops. Don't worry. I was just so lucky, and I'll be back at the pool and flying next week, I'm sure. We'll be busier than ever ferrying replacement planes. Wouldn't it be great to fly them over France?'

That prospect did not fill Francis with enthusiasm. When Arabella had informed him of Amber's crash he felt sick, and his heart thudded uncomfortably in his chest. Her reassurances were meant to steady him but what if, what if, what if was all he could thing of. What if she didn't make it? No – unthinkable – not his wonderful girl. Of course she would recover, back to her usual ebullient, capable best. This damn war must soon end. Then he wouldn't wait. He'd be over to England to see for himself that Amber was OK and Lucinda could go hang it if she objected.

Arabella and Bridie were the best nurses ever, and having Robert as her own personal doctor must have helped. Francis's heart began to return to normal and with a sigh he turned to the armament order for the American forces fighting in the Pacific.

Amber's return to duty went seamlessly. She passed her medical and was soon back to 'chits.'
Her report was accepted. Her record showed –
Pilot crash landed plane owing to zero visibility caused by heavy fog. The pilot showed exceptional skill.
Plane W.O. (Write Off)

Honor had remained at the cottage, and they slotted back into their easy camaraderie. It was great to share daily experiences as they sat together after supper. The Spitfires still rolled off the production lines and were still a joy to fly, sadly only to the RAF stations in England. They both longed to fly over to France but it was still deemed out of the question by the A.T.A. with only fewer pools cleared to do so.

Summer gave way to a golden Autumn and the land around Courtneys glowed with its golden harvest. Whenever they could she and Honor drove over. They joined the Land Girls wearing overalls, blouses, and boots to bring in the wheat harvest. They yarned together over enamel mugs of tea, homemade lemonade, and hearty sandwiches. A crisp apple kept them going.

Amber most enjoyed the rhythm of forking the stooks of corn into the hopper of the threshing machine, which chugged happily. Honor preferred seeing the golden grains emerge from the chute into the sacks. She was quick at changing to a new bag and tying off the full one. She hadn't been a farmer's daughter in the Mid-West for nothing.

A quick supper enjoyed with Arabella and Robert, then it was back to the pool, or an overnight stay when they giggled together like schoolgirls in Amber's big bed.

It was great to be tired and a bit sore after a full day of physical work.   The land girls never tired of asking them about their lives in America.   Was it dead glamorous?   Did they ever meet Clark Gable, who was supposed to be over in England?   Did they get stockings and lipstick sent over from home?   Were they ever scared when they flew their planes? What did they think of English boys 'Cos we think they're dead boring?

Amber dare not tell them that she part-owned a Hollywood studio, or they would all want screen tests after the war.

The Allies were advancing steadily against a determined enemy, but with superior air power, held a mighty advantage.

Eddy wrote to her with the now familiar black scored words. Amber longed to see him.   Each time she looked at the Hoppner Painting she felt a deep need to see the curly-haired child now grown into manhood.   Would they walk together, then sit as she made a daisy chain for him to loop in her hair?   Weren't they too old for such playful games? 'Just let him come back,' she prayed.

Honor and Uncle Hubert joined them for a Courtneys Christmas.   The girls had been lucky enough to be given 48 hours leave.

Honor and Hubert developed a keen chess rivalry, with Robert and Hubert savouring the cellar ports over some fine estate cheeses, all went well.

The traditional midnight service at ancient St Barts, with hot punch on their return set the tone for a happy two days of celebrations.

Arabella had sung her two great solos - 'I know that my Redeemer liveth' and 'Silent Night.' Yet it was a schoolboy treble singing 'Away in a Manger' that caused a sensation.

Perhaps St. Bart's had nurtured another singing star.

Germany was, by the early spring of 1945, on the verge of defeat. Russia had seen off Hitler's ill-judged invasion. Italy had capitulated, and Mussolini was dead. The American Eighth Army Airforce Flying Fortresses and the British Lancasters had devastated dozens of German cities. The German surrender was not long delayed, and the hated Hitler had committed suicide.

VE day left the Allies victorious and jubilant, while the Germans set about rebuilding their country under the occupation of their conquerors.

The A.T.A. had been slowly winding down as most of the overseas pilots had been returning home as their contracts ended. The proud total for the pilots was 308,567 planes ferried.   They had given it their best shot since the A.T.A. formation.   They had freed up fighting pilots and helped to win the war.   Their pools had lost comrades who would not be forgotten.

Each A.T.A. pilot left with as little fuss as when they had first joined.   Just a firm handshake and 'Well done and thank you,' as is the British way.   They had been heroic.

After four years of flying, Honor and Amber's contracts had ended.   They had joined up as willing volunteers, been treated and paid equally to the men, endured hardship, and danger, and done the job.   They clung together in a hug, promising to keep in touch.

Amber realised that she had changed so completely during her A.T.A. years.   She was no longer the Grantley heiress and indulged princess.   She had faced up to taking orders, and the daily risks of wartime flying.   She had emerged stronger, and a little humbler faced with the courage of the Brits around her and somehow, yes somehow English herself.

Amber had decided to stay in England for a while longer with her English family.   In truth she wanted to be within reach of Eddy.

He had completed his posting to set up advanced airfields as the Allies pressed forward into Germany.   Now he had been sent to join a team to seek out German jet and rocket planes and their technology. Also to locate, dismantle and send back to Britain any wind tunnels, which were in short supply at home.

His letters had been necessarily short of info. She read them again and again and treasured their 'With love Eddy' endings. Couldn't he say, 'With All my love' or 'Missing you dreadfully?'

Amber so longed for him, and his return couldn't come a moment too soon.

Meanwhile she luxuriated in an English summer. Day after sunlit day was spent working in the rose garden with Arabella. The very roses which old Archibald Finch, the late head gardener, had toiled and sworn profanities over. The roses where her American grandfather had worked with old Finch in contentment and accord.

The perfect rose which Finch had propagated for Miss Arabella was in full bloom and was the glory of the garden, not only perfectly formed, but with the most glorious subtle perfume.

Amber was restless but full of energy. She was no longer flying, and decided with Arabella, to embark on a new project. Calls went out to Grantleys (London) and soon a delivery arrived. Bridie helped to unpack the boxes.

'Oh Miss Amber, what are ye about?'

'I'll leave all the house to you and Mom, but this is going to be my project.'

So, wearing her oldest pair of flying overalls, and with her hair tied up in a turban like all the wartime factory girls, she and John Webster looked out two ladders.

'Do be careful Miss Amber.   Why don't you let one of the lads do it?'

'Don't worry Bridie.   I'm used to heights you know, and Mom and I want to do this.   We'll need you to help with lots of tea, coffee, and cake to keep us going.'

With that she was up the ladder to inspect the tiles on the roof of the pavilion which had played such a big part in Francis's life.   It was where he had spied the young Arabella and painted her.   It was where he had spent many hours sitting then painting again as he recuperated from his Great War incarceration.   Now during the years of this war, it had become faded and shabby so Amber would bring it back to life just as Arabella had brought Francis back to life.   It held so many memories, and she wanted to be creating her own there with Eddy.

She cleaned off all the old moss and dead leaves from the tiles and the drainpipes.   Then she started on the real grind of rubbing down all the old paint on the wooden plank walls. It was jolly hard work, but she revelled in the physical effort. As each board shed its tired old flaking paint and emerged smooth and eager for its new livery, she felt she was helping an old friend to new life.

It took day after day, but she persevered, working off aching muscles in arms, legs and back, for good preparation, in painting as in flying, results in a good finish. Three panes of cracked glass were replaced and as she began to undercoat the blue and white pavilion, the boxes' contents were fully revealed.

Arabella joined her in happy accord while she emptied the inside of the pavilion entirely. How could so much rubbish and so many useless odds and ends have collected?

With Bridie's help the inside was transformed into a clean fresh-smelling welcoming space. All the old junk went to the garden bonfire.

Bridie's voice rang out with,
'She is handsome, she is pretty
She's the belle of Dublin City
She's a courtin' one, two three (with three claps)
Please won't you tell me
Who is she?'

Arabella joined in with the next chorus then they fell about laughing. Joy and laughter were returning to Courtneys after the dark days of war.

With a final flourish of Amber's paint brush, they stood back to admire the results of their efforts. It all looked so splendid that they decided on a re-opening ceremony the very next day.

Four new Lloyd Loom chairs had been found. One long table held crockery, cutlery, and glasses, while on the opposite side stood a table holding all Francis's and Robert's paints, brushes, and palettes.

The heady aroma of roses filled the air. The sun shone down approvingly as Amber cut the ribbon and declared the pavilion officially re-opened. The three of them had established new ties and as the 'Three Musketeers' served beer and coffee (Grantleys again) and tea and strong whiskey cake to all the gardeners and staff. Micky felt old. He had arrived at Courtneys as a young lad with his older brothers. He'd taken to the horses, and Old Finch too. Now _he_ was the old retainer with his gammy leg and only a couple of horses to tend. Miss Arabella had told him that he would always be welcome to stay in the stable flat, and only to do what he felt able. Sure, hadn't it been a lucky day when his Aunt Bridie had brought them over from Ireland? He wasn't too old to slip a drop of the good stuff to a couple of the

lads, just to keep them all going.   Sure, weren't Courtneys
and Miss Arabella just the best?

CHAPTER 38
LOVE IS A MANY SPLENDOURED THING

Amber took her breakfast out to the pavilion and read Robert's morning paper.   She had her usual book of British History and persuaded herself that she was becoming something of an expert on the subject.

When Arabella joined her, they walked in the vegetable garden admiring all the produce, then set to, to clear a spent bed and prepare it for its next planting.

'You know Mom, I reckon this could be a real commercial part of the estate.   During the war everyone 'Dug for Victory,' now they want their lawns back and a bit of leisure, but they'll need to be buying fruit and vegetables.'

'You could be right.   Let's talk to Robert and Steve Maitland at the next Estate's meeting.'

After lunch Arabella retired to practice her vocal exercises, while Amber changed into a cool summer dress.   She had taken to cycling around the estate on voyages of discovery. As she collected her bike Bridie rushed out with a message. Could Amber please call at Deacon's Farm late afternoon?

'Sure thing,' said Amber to a sparkling Bridie.
'See you later then.'

She cycled at a comfortable pace, stopping to sit by a favourite stream to check for tadpoles or small fish. Then a call to Seal's farm for a cool drink of lemonade and a chat with Mrs. Seal. A warm scone was happily consumed. The estate tenants had come to know Amber. They had admired her uniform and the work she did to help England during the war. No-one had made her leave America and her wealthy and safe life there with Mr Francis and her American family. Shame that her Dad and Mum had divorced. He'd been so good to them all and kept helping Miss Arabella to keep the estate going. Miss Amber would inherit it all, so stood to sense that she wanted to get to know them.

As they shared their drinks, Mrs Seal said,
'Lovely summer we're havin Miss. 'Speck you'll be sad to leave it when you go back home to America.'
Did she hesitate before answering?
'It is lovely and I'm enjoying every day, so I don't feel like rushing back. I do miss Dad when I'm here but in America I'll miss Mom and Courtneys and all of you.'

Mrs Seal noticed that Amber had a catch in her voice and looked at her keenly as she patted her arm before seeing her on her way.

By the time she reached Deacon's, the land girls who were still working there, had called in the cows for milking. There was just one solitary figure forking hay from a rick. He was naked to the waist and had his back to her. She slipped her arms around his waist. He smelt of drying sweat, Imperial Leather brilliantine overlaid with sweet aroma of hay, and a smell of masculinity which excited her. He turned and folded her in his arms.

'Oh Amber – at last. After so very long we've made it.'

Their kisses were sweet. He thought you could always tell a girl's character by her kisses. Hers were pure heaven. He had plucked his Cloud 9 girl at last from the skies down to this earthly paradise.

She wore a floaty cotton dress in sky blue and very little else. Their union was so natural. Here were two bodies which belonged together. They met in joyful congress. No aggressive macho assertion, just the sure knowledge that Eddy would carry her with him on their wonderful journey of discovering her secret places and giving them both the most intense pleasure.

Eddy had made love – no been intimate with – plenty of girls. Now he knew what making love really meant. It meant giving every particle of himself freely, expressed in the time-honoured ceremony of joining their bodies and their destinies together.

At last, as they lay wonderfully spent among the hay with her

head resting on his chest, Eddy said,
'Will you marry me, Amber? As soon as possible please!
Let's not waste any more time. It will take the rest of our
lives to enjoy our marriage, have our children, three at least,
and make a home and living for us all.'

Amber needed to tell him – and very soon – of her life in
America and her work with Grantley Air Corporation. Yet
not today. Never ever to change these magic hours with
uncertainty. Tomorrow would be soon enough.

This golden evening and starlit night must be perfect.

They cycled back to Courtneys to find that Arabella and
Robert had retired to the Dower House. Bridie had
disappeared to a stable flat but left a note
SUPPER IS ON THE KITCHEN TABLE.

After the swiftest of washes and change of clothes, they ate
omelettes made with the freshest of eggs together with tiny
salad potatoes and the crispest of salads. There was sliced
ham with pickles and fresh bread, then cheese and golden
apples. Amber even sipped a little of Eddy's beer. HORRID!

Clever Bridie had managed to make sure they had met in the
most carefree of settings. Did the 'cheeky minx' know what
would happen next?

They just stacked the dishes, checked the locks and headed upstairs.   Eddy carried her over the bedroom threshold. They stood with arms entwined and gazed at 'their' portrait.

Eddy turned to her, took both her hands in his and said, 'I love you Amber Seymour, I love you with every particle of my being.   There's no song or poem that even begins to explain it.   Even my Irish minstrel forbears couldn't.   So come kiss me and let's to bed.'

Amber resolutely refused to allow herself any comparison between Eddy and Max.   Perhaps you could only make love completely when you loved and desired someone utterly.

She thought of all the Courtney women who had lain in this bedroom.   Some young brides, some like her a little older, and perhaps marrying for the second time.   Yet all hoping for the devotion which she was enjoying.

Flying had always filled her life.   Now she had a life force to satisfy her body, father her future children and fill her life with his own brand of lively joy.

How very strange that she who flew virtually every day had rarely even thought of it during these long summer days at Courtneys.

With the end of her A.T.A. contract had come the end of her

obsession with flying.

If 'The Night has a thousand eyes,' several of them might have popped when looked in through Amber's open windows.

At last, banished by the sunrise the stars took their leave. Amber woke, stretched, and gazed at her love. He lay like a curly-haired cupid. Dimpled in sleep, with long dark eyelashes, she kissed him back to wakefulness, and the certain knowledge that he would be up – literally – to make love to her or she to him again.

Glowing with delight she walked naked to open the doors for cook, the maids and dear Bridie. She must make sure that Eddy saw his mother frequently and that Arabella was no longer denied her home.

They took their breakfast to the pavilion. Eddy ate copious amounts of toast and honey and drank cup after cup of tea. Amber sipped her coffee nervously and realised that she could not delay the conversation any longer…………

'Bridie knows, but I guess she hasn't told you about my life in America. You know me as Amber Seymour, but I married under my real name of Amber Grantley. You met my father, Francis, and all the family before we left in 1913 for America, when I was just a baby. I grew up at Fairhaven, the large family compound with Grandfather Randolph and Grandmother Dorothea. Mom was often away touring her operas or here at Courtneys after the war.

My Aunt Philly taught me to drive and race cars. My Aunt Netty taught me to fly and the management of Grantley Aeroplane Company for when I took over from her. Neither Aunt has any children so I expect I shall inherit their estates. When Grandmother died, she left Fairhaven, not to Pop and his new wife, but to me. It means that am a wealthy woman but with a whole cartload of responsibilities in America. Pops is tired out and should have retired years ago. He is expecting me back now the war is over.

What shall we do? Shall we –
Marry here and just visit America on honeymoon?
Marry here, honeymoon here, then go to America?
Marry here, stay here to help Mom and Bridie and Steve Maitland manage the estate?'

Eddy's face had become sombre as she made her confession. He now remembered the confident men and women who had come to Courtneys and taken Amber away with them. Then when she had come to fly for England, he only met her on the day she married his best friend. He could not bear to lose her again. Yet she was hugely wealthy, while he would return to being a country solicitor. Would it be enough? Could he stand being a kept man? Robert and Arabella seemed to have managed their marriage splendidly.   He must take lessons from Robert.

Amber laid her head on his chest and looked at him enquiringly.   Seizing her hand, he said fiercely.
'I don't give a hang about any of it except that we live together, work together, and spend our lives together, the way that the painter wanted the children in his picture to live happily ever after.   Can I show you something?'

Keeping her hand tightly clasped in his they walked through to the stables.   A noisy cacophany of yelps and barks issued from one stall.   Here a small ginger dog was trying to control her litter of five frisky puppies.   One of them gave several little yaps of greeting and ran to snuffle Amber's shoes.   This was the line of pups bred from his first dog Flossie.   He lifted the little chap into Amber's arms.

'Do you see darling, it's really about generation to generation.   What will you call him?'

'I think I'll decide when I get to know him better,' she replied stroking the little head and looking into alert bright eyes.

Then Eddy took her to the paddock where she had last walked, on the fog shrouded day when she crash landed. There was a splendid mare with a fine foal at heel.   The great stallion watching the scene from the stable door must be the progeny of the mighty Raven, then Wing, then who knows? Only Micky who kept the stud book. The bloodlines went right back to the spectacular horse which an earlier Courtney had presented to King Charles II. Micky had left the new foal for Amber and Arabella to name.

Amber at once understood. She heard the whispers of her ancestors calling in her blood. Now she knew what she must do. Turning to Eddy she said,
'Let's get married quickly and quietly. Then you'll be demobbed. We could take a boat to America, and meet them all – Pops, Lucinda, Johnie, the aunts, and uncles, all of them.
Pops and the aunts want to retire from Grantley Corporation, and so do I. I'll be pregnant by then, and our child, like us, must be born at Courtneys. What do you say Eddy?'

'Hey, slow down, give a chap time to digest all that,' he laughed.
'Sounds terrific – we'll work on it.'

Mother and foal trotted over to be fed one of Finch's golden apples each. The stallion tossed his head and snorted in dismay.
'Don't worry old chap, we haven't forgotten you. It's your progeny who are going to help me get the Courtney stud going again. Your name and your foals will be famous

throughout the land.'

With a re-assuring pat, they left the 'Gret black hoss' as Finch always called him.

'Now who's making plans,' teased Amber as they walked slowly back to the house.

CHAPTER 39
AMBER AND EDDY

Amber and Eddy were married in the same Catholic church where his mother, Bridie, had married Dr. Daniels.

The wedding was as they had requested, low key yet strangely beautiful.   Only Arabella and Robert, Bridie and Robert's friend, Dr. Peter Jameson, together with Captain Stuart Gregory, the best man, were present.

When consulted by the priest as to their intentions for the spiritual care of any children, the couple agreed that they would be brought up in the Catholic faith.   Amber didn't really care as long as there were children of the marriage. She and Eddy could provide a loving home where they would not be spoiled by wealth or privilege.   There would be all the outdoor activities they could cram into a day.   The children would attend the village school, and their chums would be the village and estate children.

When Amber entered the church expecting to be escorted down the aisle by Robert, she had a wonderful surprise. Awaiting her arrival stood a tall, thin, grey-haired gentleman who kissed her on the cheek and offering his arm escorted her down the aisle to her bridegroom.   He had said only two words –
'Darling Amber.' While she replied –

'Thank you, Pops, oh thank you so very much.'

With hearts brimming with happiness, everyone seemed to emanate a special glow.   Even the priest officiating was hard pressed not to smile too much.   The photographs were quickly taken, and in later years the tall handsome RAF officer, the glowing bride, her proud Papa with Arabella, and Robert at one end and Bridie with Peter at the other drew admiring comments.

The wedding breakfast was another example of cook's expertise and was held at the Dower House.   This time Messrs Fortnum and Mason were able to assist and to supply the wedding cake which was cut with due ceremony.   The speeches were short, but heart felt, none more so than Francis's tribute to his beautiful, talented, and brave daughter.

As Eddy drove them away in Amber's sports car with a jolly toot on the horn, all agreed it had been the perfect wedding.

After her wedding night Amber knew that she had the perfect husband,
Wow, Wow, and Wow!

CHAPTER 40

Francis stayed with Arabella and Robert for three days. They had much to discuss and catch up on. There was surprisingly little awkwardness. Too many years had passed since the divorce and Francis was happy to be back at the great house and estate which he had helped Arabella to save, and which his allowances still supported.

The men painted together in amicable near silence. Bridie and her doctor friend joined them for supper each evening. The men played billiards with much laughter at their incompetence, while Arabella and Bridie just sat and enjoyed it all.

Arabella saw how the second war he had worked through had weakened Francis. When he left to join Lucinda who had stayed in London, she hugged him warmly.
'Thank you, dear Francis for everything. You've always been so good to me, and we'll be close through Amber and fond memories.'

Francis looked at her so searchingly as if to commit every part of her to memory.
'They were the best of times, and I'll never forget. Be happy, my very dear Arabella. Look after our daughter and the children to come.
God bless you all.'

With his final kiss and a small bow, he joined Robert in the car for the drive to the station.   He did not look back.

Arabella was quite overcome by her emotions and wept quietly.   Then she pulled herself together and went to look at the painting on his easel in the garden pavilion.

It was of a young woman with golden hair.   She was bending over a dark, curly-haired boy and a blond girl with a daisy chain in her hair.
The woman was looking up at the painter.   She had deep violet eyes which told of music and love and laughter.
Arabella held it to her heart for Francis had painted his enduring love for her.

Why on earth had she ever left Francis?   The answer as always lay before her.   While she lived, Courtneys would claim her.   She had not been born into the family, but she had devoted her life to saving their home.   By her strange violent coupling with Richard Courtney, she had ensured that the blood line would continue through Amber and her children down the years.

Amber's cable reached her mother.   By agreement she had not telephoned during her honeymoon.   That was for lovers, not chatting to parents.
It read –
    Dear Mama and Robert

We'll be home very soon.   Sailing on the QM.   Can't wait to
see you both.   Have cabled Bridie.
Home is where the heart is, and we realise this is with you all
at Courtneys.

Love, love and love
Amber and Eddy

So that decided it!
A large banner hung across the portico.   It read –
WELCOME Home Mr and Mrs QUINLAN

Eddy carried his wife, AMBER, AURELIA DOROTHEA, EVELYN
QUINLAN over the threshold of the house they loved.

They breathed in its air with relish.   It smelt of polish and
flowers and the years of its existence.   The library
contributed with the faint smell of leather-bound volumes.
There was the merest whisper of whiskey from the cake laid
out in the small sitting room.   The sweet aroma of the apple
logs burning in the grate reached them   It smelt of a home
and love and a future with no war to cloud the horizon.

'Hello, we're home' they called.   Only then did Amber see
the large envelope addressed to her and Eddy.

Arabella had written –
'Darlings – welcome home.   We hope you have had the most
marvellous time.   Our wedding gift to you both surrounds

you. Courtneys is passed to you now to care for – to love –
to raise your family and to be so happy. Robert and I are
contented in the Dower House, and Bridie has moved into a
cottage in the village.
Cook and all the staff remain to support you.
All we ask is that you include the name Courtney for each of
your children.

Love and Love,
                    Mama and Robert
                              Xx

COURTNEYS WAS THEIRS!

They walked to the stables to give a golden apple to each of
the horses. The foal had grown so much and would be a
fine animal. The stallion munched his apple and looked on
approvingly. As soon as the mare returned to her owners,
he'd be out in the paddock preparing for his next
appointment. Even better than an apple!

The puppy ran to Amber, and she swept him up into her
arms.

'I'll call him Brandy. Let's take him up to the house for a
while, can we?'

Brandy frolicked around the kitchen before falling asleep

against the warmth of the range.   They ate the meal cook
had left warming for them.
Then they walked over in the dusk to thank Arabella from full
hearts.   They needed to be sure that she and Robert were
happy in the Dower House, for Courtneys was big enough for
them all.

'Just fill it with children, for I couldn't.   That's all we ask,'
said Arabella.

They laughed together at this delightful prospect.   The talk
turned to Fairhaven after their visit, and to America at large.

Amber explained that the aunts and uncles were now over
80 and a little frail.   The estate was as huge and lavish as
before.   Amber had been inspired by the gardens and had
enjoyed the picture gallery.

Eddy had flown Grantley planes from their airfield, but
astonishingly Amber seemed to have lost all interest.
The aunts looked at each other knowingly and mouthed
PREGNANT!

Amber and Eddy had both found America a little over
whelming.   It's people were self-confident and exuberant,
and there were no shortages.

After war-torn, shabby, and still rationed England the

comparisons had been startling and unsettling.

Born in England, Amber had been uprooted to America as a baby and had grown up and embraced life there. Yet when Britain had called for American volunteers to fly for the A.T.A., she had immediately uprooted to go and help.

Now here she was, back with her beloved Eddy, at their beautiful Courtneys.
A Yankee turned English rose. How old Archie Finch would have approved. Just so long as she tended the danged roses, and the 'Gret black hoss' kept them well manured!

CHAPTER 41
BRIDIE – Has the last word

So here we are, Miss Arabella and Mr Robert have both retired, and I've been pensioned off. It's a great pension too and a free cottage for life.

My Eddy and Miss Amber are taking over the big house, though I expect they'll be visiting the Dower House every day, and vice versa.

It's a big change for me as well. I've always worked, mainly for Miss Arabella. We've seen some times together, sure we have. Not quite rags to riches but she started as a house maid, then worked till she could hardly stand, let alone sing, to earn the money to buy Courtneys off that Richard Courtney, with his drinking and gambling and loose women. If he had turned out different, he could have married Miss Arabella, but drink does for the best, and then she went and saved his life. She's good at that is Miss Arabella, cos then her and me had to save Mr Francis when he came back from the war like a skeleton.

She saw the world with me when she was touring and singing, and we both learned a lot. O' course her Daddy was Irish. Sure, hadn't he the looks and blarney to charm the birds off the trees, and any woman into his bed.

Now my Eddy is married to Miss Amber, so there's my Irish

blood as well.   Old Finch used to call me 'That cheeky Irish minx,' and I've still a roguish eye.

Dr Peter is my gentleman caller.   He's welcome to visit, but I'm not for marrying again.   Twice was quite enough, and I want to stay close to Courtneys to mind me grandchildren. Sure, we've had some grand times and there'll be a lot more before I've finished.

There's no-one knows more about running the house, so they'll be asking me questions when I'm in me rocking chair!

No one can believe that Miss Amber has given up on flying. It's been her life's blood for over twenty years since she was a little lass.

Perhaps it's flying all those different planes day in and day out when she came to join the A.T.A.   It's men and women like her who helped us to beat that raving lunatic Hitler with his plans to take us all over.   He'd obviously never heard us sing 'Britons never, never, will be slaves,' and that definitely includes the Irish.

She always looked ever so smart in her uniform, and I bless the day she decided to come back to England and to my Eddy.   Theirs is a match made in heaven if you like.   They were always up in the clouds.   Now she's to buy up loads more land to extend the estate and tend the gardens till they'll be the glory of the county.

My Eddy'll have paddocks and stables galore, and the knowledge that every true Irishman has of horses will keep him and old Micky busy.

When I go back up to Courtneys for a cup of tea with cook it's like a mad house.   There's dogs running in and out, and folk in and out after tea or coffee all day.   Nancy's got some sense.   She set up one of the sculleries as a Tea Room.   They have to make their own and wash up after or she withdraws her cakes and biscuits.   I've had to give her the recipe for me Irish whiskey cake which went against the grain, but Courtneys would fall apart without it.

What a year!   Peace at last, then the wedding and now Christmas is nearly on us.   The majesty and traditions will be just as wonderful as ever.   Miss Amber has asked Miss Arabella and me to help with it all, especially the foliage and flowers and fruit and candles.   Won't that be great?   For she's never done any housekeeping until she came here. Cook's trying to teach her basic cooking, but its hard work. She gave up with Christmas pudding, and mince pies defeated her.   There'll be me and me fancy man, and all the staff and the family.   They've invited Sir Hubert.   Him and Mr Robert 'll be polishing off the port, then snoring in their armchairs.   It'll be hard to find a gift for everybody but my Eddy's on to it.   Knowing him they'll each get a bottle of Irish whiskey.   Knowing Miss Amber, all the women will be spoilt with nylons and posh perfume.   Though Nancy 'ud prefer some sensible lisle stockings and a tub of Ponds Cold Cream. As long as Sir Hubert gets his box of Cuban cigars, he'll be happy – even though the smoke ruins Miss Arabella's voice.

We've turkeys and pheasants, and all manner of vegs, fruits and hams and cheeses, so we'll not starve.   It's grand how it's all come together.

We'll all troop off to St Bart's for Christmas Eve service, then back for hot punch and mince pies.   We'll sing 'Hark the Herald Angels Sing' and be thankful that there is 'Peace on Earth and Mercy Mild' – though I still don't feel very peaceful towards them Germans.

We'll celebrate the year ahead.   1946 will see the birth of the first grandchild for Miss Arabella and me.   Bet we get to name him.   How about Archie Francis Sean?   Then that old rascal Archibald Finch 'll live on in the lad.

Courtneys will do what its hus always done and enfold us all.

The child will be born, live, and likely die here.   Just another generation to cherish.   On they'll go with their busy lives, while Courtneys holds them, and warms them and protects them, and goes on forever.

FRANCIS EDWARD COURTNEY QUINLAN   b 1946

ARCHIE ROBERT COURTNEY QUINLAN   b 1948

DOROTHEA ANNE COURTNEY QUINLAN   b 1950

HUBERT SEAN COURTNEY QUINLAN   b 1953

ACKNOWLEDGEMENTS

My gratitude for their unfailing support and encouragement goes to:

VAL   - Proof reader and so much more to keep the narrative credible.

TONY   - Expert on all things relating to Aviation and with a large collection of books on the subject.

SHARON   - Speed typist and effective reader of my handwriting.

PENNY   - Ready, as always, with speedy answers to my questions.

DAVID   - Successful author whose expertise is invaluable and punctuation impeccable.

BEN   - Who knocks it all into shape to produce the book.

You are all terrific!

Printed in Great Britain
by Amazon

54790579R00150